FLAVOURS OF HACKNEY

Born and raised in east London, Leke Apena graduated from the University of Brighton in 2011 with a degree in English Language and pursued a career in communications. He writes unconventional, challenging and entertaining stories about the modern Black British experience.

Follow Leke on social media

Instagram: @urbanintellectual

Twitter: @LekeApena

Other books by the same author

A Prophet Who Loved Her

LEKE APENA

FLAVOURS OF HACKNEY

Printed and bound by
Lighting Source UK Ltd
Milton Keynes, MK11 3LW

For my daughter

Prologue

July 2007

When it came to who was better at basketball, Jamal was clearly superior. By a country mile. But Gavin would never admit it with his stubborn, big head. So Jamal would just have to embarrass him again.

Like he always did.

On a bright summer afternoon in Brixton, it was the hottest day of the year so far as July came to a close. 11-year-old Jamal Jones and his best friend, Gavin Campbell, were shooting hoops in a caged basketball court on Angell Town estate. They were the only boys in the cage today. Low-rise, brown-bricked council flats surrounded them. Tall, leafy trees stood over the metal cage with their long, thick branches and lush, green leaves, giving their rough, concrete environment some much needed greenery and life.

Jamal stood behind Gavin. Today, Jamal wore his Arsenal jersey with the surname 'Walcott', his favourite Arsenal forward, printed at the back. He watched as Gavin stood facing the basketball hoop a few feet away at the end of the court, bouncing the brown basketball in his hands. Jamal smirked as Gavin took a deep breath, bent his knees and threw the ball towards the net. At first, the basketball made a promising arch towards the net. But it quickly lost momentum and nosedived to the ground, merely brushing the end of the net instead.

"Argh, man, allow it," Gavin moaned, kicking his foot against the ground.

"Ok, lemme show you how you actually shoot, innit," Jamal said, shoving Gavin lightly on the shoulder.

Gavin kissed his teeth. "Whatever, man."

Jamal dashed over to the corner of the cage where the basketball had rolled. He picked it up, and the ball felt so right between his hands as if they were specifically created by God for the sole purpose of playing basketball. Bouncing the ball confidently,

Jamal made his way to the middle of the court. Gavin stood back as Jamal looked at the hoop at the end of the court. He bounced the ball on the ground, preparing for the right moment to take his shot.

"Watch, I bet you miss, innit," Gavin said from behind him.

But Jamal rarely threw a crap shot. His mouth curved into a grin, and he bent his knees slightly. With some force from his feet and steady hands, he launched the basketball into the air. The basketball made one smooth arch through the air before swooping perfectly through the net. Kobe Bryant would have approved.

Gavin shook his head in disbelief but Jamal could tell he was also impressed. "Nah, but how do you never miss, man?" Gavin said as Jamal skipped to the front of the court to collect the basketball. "Bruv, when we start year 7, you gotta join the school's basketball team."

Jamal jogged back to Gavin, bouncing the basketball between his legs. "Yeah, I probably will.

But I was also thinking about joining a Pokémon club or something."

Gavin raised his eyebrows and looked at Jamal as if he had said he wanted to kiss his pet hamster. "A Pokémon club?" he said with exaggerated disgust. "Mate, we're going to year 7 now. You gotta allow the Pokémon cards. That's for neeks, you get me."

Jamal stopped bouncing the basketball and held it by his side. He regarded his best friend and shook his head. "Why do you hate Pokémon so much? But you like Dragonball Z ?"

"Erm…because Dragonball Z is actually sick," Gavin said, stretching his arms and shrugging his shoulders as if to say that was obvious. "Bruv, are you gonna go into year 7 and tell everyone you play with Pokémon cards? You ain't gonna get no girls doing that. You think *gash* like boys who still play Pokémon?"

The topic of girls lit up Jamal's face. Of course, he was excited to be starting secondary school with Gavin and their other friends from primary school. Still, he was more intrigued by the fact he would be seeing girls he had never seen before. There would be different types of girls than those he had seen at primary school such as teenage girls wearing skirts, lipstick and makeup. Just thinking about it produced a stupid grin on Jamal's face.

"Man, I can't wait to meet the girls," Jamal said, already daydreaming as he looked up at the clear sky. "Like we're gonna be seeing fifteen-year-olds and sixteen-year-olds. Proper tings, man."

"I know, man" Gavin said, looking like he was also daydreaming as he looked upwards. He then screwed his face and twisted his lips as if something bitter had entered his mouth. "But we're gonna be like the youngers at school now, innit. So the older tings ain't gonna ask us out." Gavin had a defeated look on his face. "The older girls are gonna say we're like their little brothers." He put on a mock impersonation of an older teenage girl. "Aww, you're so cute." Gavin shook his head. "It's deep, man."

Jamal chuckled and punched Gavin lightly on the shoulder. "I bet you ain't gonna chat to any tings on the first day anyway."

Gavin scrunched his face defensively. "What are you on about? Bruv, I am gonna chat to bare gash."

"Really? Ok then. If I draw more girls than you on the first day, then you have to let me keep GTA Vice City."

"I can't believe you're still playing that game," Gavin said, shaking his head at Jamal. "You do know GTA San Andreas has been out for time? You're bare late, bruv."

"Whatever, man. Don't change the subject, innit. Do we have a deal or not?" Jamal extended his right hand in front of Gavin.

Gavin grinned at Jamal and shook his hand. "Yeah, we got a deal. I am telling you now, though, you won't draw more tings than me on the first day. Even if you prayed to God, bruv."

Jamal ended their handshake and scoffed. "Whatever, man. We'll see, innit."

Before either of them could continue debating who was more skilled at talking to girls, a familiar voice echoed over the court.

"Gavin, can you come home now. We're going to Brixton market. I am buying some plantain, and I need you to help me carry the bags."

Gavin looked up and saw his mother, Shanice Campbell, wearing her blue headscarf, sticking her head out the window of the second-floor council flat Gavin called home. The apartment was directly opposite the caged basketball court.

"Come on, mum," Gavin shouted back with a moan. He slapped his hands on his legs as he threw a mini tantrum. "I am playing basketball with Jamal, man."

"Do I look like I give a rass, Gavin," Shanice said, glowering at him. "Get your butt up here now!" Shanice then looked at Jamal, and her entire demeanour transformed instantly. "Hello, Jamal. Say hello to your mum for me."

"Yes, I will, auntie," Jamal said, waving back at Gavin's mum with a smile.

When Shanice disappeared from the window, retreating back into the flat, Gavin turned back to Jamal. He sighed and dragged his right hand down his face. "Why is my mum so annoying, man. Anyway, I'll catch you later, innit. Safe."

"Yeah, safe." Jamal and Gavin did their signature handshake, which involved slapping each other's palms twice and then finishing it by bashing each other's knuckles.

As Gavin dragged himself out of the court, Jamal turned around, grinned at his best friend, and called at him loudly as he walked off. "And don't forget our bet, bruv."

Now by the cage's door, Gavin turned around and smirked at Jamal. "I ain't gonna forget. But bruv, I beg you throw away those Pokémon cards, or you'll never get a wifey."

Jamal laughed and turned his attention to the basketball net as Gavin left the cage. He bounced the basketball on the ground a few times before launching the ball at the net. Another perfect shot.

Before Jamal could walk to the end of the court to collect the basketball, he felt someone tap his shoulder in a panic. He swiftly turned around. To Jamal's surprise, Gavin was standing behind him. A look of grave concern hardened his best friend's features. Jamal instantly knew something was wrong.

"What's up, bruv?" Jamal said, raising his eyebrows at Gavin. "You look mad shook."

Gavin opened his mouth to speak, but Jamal had already looked over Gavin's shoulders and clocked the three boys in all black tracksuits entering the cage. Despite having their hoodies over their heads, resembling three grim reapers, Jamal could tell that the boys were black. They strutted towards Jamal and Gavin, walking as if they had a limp, and their tracksuit bottoms were worn low enough that you could see the top half of their boxers. Jamal knew these boys were not here for a friendly game of basketball. Growing up in Angell Town estate had given him a sixth sense to detect trouble.

The three boys in tracksuits stood before Jamal and Gavin, invading their personal space like a virus. Standing so close to them, Jamal realised the boys were maybe three years older than himself and Gavin. Their body frames were leaner and taller. The boy in the middle, who was the tallest and wore black Nike gloves, glared at the two of them and spoke first. "Blud, which one of you is Jamal? Kieran's younger brother?"

It was both a question and a threat. But Jamal was not shaken, and he raised his chin at the three boys and deepened his voice. "Yeah, I am Kieran's brother. And what?"

In a flash, all three boys pounced on Jamal. An angry shout flew from Gavin's mouth as he was shoved away by one of the boys. The boy wearing the Nike gloves swung his right fist at Jamal, but he evaded it by jumping back. From Jamal's left side, the other boy tried to grab Jamal by the sleeve, but he slapped his hands away.

Now Jamal was doubling back as the two boys engulfed him from either side, blocking any escape.

Over the two boys' shoulders, Jamal could see Gavin tussling with the third boy. When Jamal turned his attention back to the two boys who circled him like hunters cornering their prey, he saw the deadly blade of the Rambo knife. His main attacker wielded the deadly weapon, which looked like it had sharp teeth, in his gloved right hand. Jamal widened his eyes in shock and was paralysed by fear. He had never seen a knife like that in real life.

It happened so quickly. Jamal was not given the chance to react. The Rambo knife was plunged into the side of his rib, tearing through meat before it was twisted upwards. Jamal howled in pain and despair. A sharp pain exploded through his body as the knife was violently pulled out of his body. Blood splattered the tarmac.

The boy, holding the bloody Rambo knife, turned towards the other boy, still wrestling with Gavin. "Oi, Pillz, we gotta bounce. Now!"

Jamal collapsed onto the ground. The boy struggling with Gavin shoved Gavin harshly to the side of the cage. Without so much as a glance back at Jamal, now slumped on the court floor, the three attackers sprinted from the cage, pulling their sagging tracksuit bottoms up their waists.

Turning on his side, Jamal no longer felt any strong pain but his body was sore. The bottom half of his Arsenal jersey was soaking wet. When he looked down at the bottom right of his jersey, he did not initially register the growing dark stain. He placed his hand there, winced at the stinging wound and raised his hand to his face. It was covered in his blood.

Gavin came to kneel beside him. There was a cut on his best friend's top lip. He looked down at Jamal's soaking Arsenal jersey and then at Jamal's face. Never in their six years of friendship had Jamal seen Gavin look so frightened. At that moment, it really hit home how young they both were.

"They stabbed me, bruv," Jamal said, now in shock. He began to shake as tears ran down his cheeks. "Get my mummy!"

"Mum! Anyone! Please come and help me!" Gavin screamed, cradling Jamal as he desperately scanned the surrounding area. "My friend has been stabbed. Please help me!" Gavin then looked back at Jamal. Tears had now filled his eyes. "Everything is going to be alright, bruv. Just don't leave me, yeah. Don't leave me, please."

Jamal nodded his head with a groan. "I ain't gonna leave you, man. I am still breathing, innit." But Jamal could feel every breath he was taking was a struggle. Yet he wouldn't let his life slip away. Not without a fight.

Soon, the voices of women shouting filled Jamal's ears. He recognised one of them. It was his mum. Knowing she was coming to his rescue, Jamal smiled and closed his eyes. He felt weak now and wanted to rest for a bit. Everything was going to be ok now that his mum would be with him.

But when Jamal closed his eyes, he would never open them again.

Six months later

Chapter one

A mother's desperate act of love

January 2008

Most mothers would never send their only child away. But Shanice Campbell was desperate. She had to keep Gavin, her 12-year-old son, away from Brixton.

Blood had been spilt too close to home, and she could not lose her son to the sharp edge of a blade.

It had been six months since Shanice had stood beside her closest friend and watched her friend's youngest child die before her eyes. Jamal's Arsenal jersey had been soaked in blood when his limp body on the basketball court was surrounded by distraught paramedics battling to restore his life. The sirens from the police radio cars and the ambulance could not drown out the soul-piercing scream that had howled from Jamal's mother's mouth. Raw and gut-wrenching. It would haunt Shanice for the rest of her life.

To stop the painful memory from becoming too overwhelming, Shanice took measured breaths as she turned the steering wheel of her Ford Focus into Pembury Road. She looked to her left, where Gavin, her only child, was sitting in the passenger seat. Gavin was staring out the window, dressed in a grey Nike tracksuit and wired headphones around his neck. His brown cornrows, with a smooth skin fade, was Shanice's handiwork, and the hairstyle really made her son look handsome. But Gavin's frown, which had been on his face since they had left Brixton this morning, distorted his good looks into something more dark and rageful.

Shanice sighed as she turned her eyes away from him to concentrate on the road ahead. "Please be nice when we get to your uncle Reece's place."

Gavin's frown hardened, and he let out a dismissive huff. Whenever he did that, it made him resemble his father, a useless man who had chosen to no longer be in his son's life.

"Uncle Reece can't wait to see you," Shanice continued, turning to her son again and forcing a smile on her face. "He'll take good care of you, Gavin."

Now Gavin turned to face her and gave her a look that made her feel like she was the worse mother in the world. "Whatever, innit," he said, in that indistinguishable inner-London accent that almost all boys raised in the city inherited. "If you're gonna move me out of Brixton to live in Hackney, why can't I stay with uncle Benny then? He lives here, innit."

"Because your uncle Benny is not a responsible man. Do you really want to live with a man who smokes all the time and goes partying every goddamn day surrounded by party girls, even at his big age?"

Gavin looked at her, eyes wide with joy as if he had been told he had the chance to receive a lifetime supply of the latest Nike trainers. "That's a trick question," Shanice quickly added.

"Uncle Reece is so boring, man. I don't like him, innit."

"Hey, watch your mouth," Shanice snapped as she turned left into a side road that led into Pembury Estate. "Your uncle Reece is doing a big favour by letting you live with him. I want you to show him the utmost respect and listen to him at all times. Do I make myself clear, Gavin?"

Gavin turned his head away from her and scrunched his face in displeasure as he looked out the window. He did not acknowledge her. Shanice could have demanded an answer but knew it would result in another argument between mother and son. Shanice let out a tired sigh.

Reece was already standing outside as Shanice pulled her car into one of the available parking bays. Once she had parked the car safely, Shanice switched off the engine and let herself out of the vehicle with Gavin doing the same.

Hackney's Pembury estate seemed more like a small village than an estate with its dozens of brown-bricked, walk-up blocks in every direction one looked. These blocks housed the many council flats and maisonettes. It felt more expansive than Brixton's Angell Town estate. Like most council estates in London, which were populated mainly by the working class and the poor, you could smell the grittiness in the air. Due to an indifferent council, this urban decay stained singled-glazed windows. It was reflected in the peeling paint on many of the flat doors. But you also felt a sense of community as washing lines hung from the balconies and the smell of home cooking weaved in the air. As Shanice walked over to Reece, she spotted two black boys, probably no older than Gavin, kicking a football and laughing with each other. This sight calmed Shanice's nerves a little. At least Gavin would find friends here.

"Look at my nephew! Seems like you've grown an extra six inches from the last time I saw you," Reece said, approaching Gavin with a wide grin on his clean-shaven face. He hugged Gavin, but Gavin stood there like his body was made from the same bricks as the blocks in the estate. Reece took no offence as he pulled back from Gavin. "Go get your stuff out of the car's boot, please." Gavin looked at his uncle with narrowed eyes and all the attitude of Bart Simpson.

Shanice cleared her throat. "You heard what your uncle said, Gavin."

Gavin mumbled something unintelligible. He then kissed his teeth, plodded to the car's boot, and lifted it up to take out his luggage. With a sigh, Shanice turned away from her son and looked at Reece. He had tied his dreadlocks into a ponytail. This bought out his chiselled cheeks and highlighted his very symmetrical face. His fashion model aesthetics had made her younger brother - Shanice was older than him by five years - fiercely popular with the ladies growing up. As a bachelor still in his early thirties, Shanice and the rest of her family always teased Reece that God was playing a cruel joke. How could someone blessed with his handsomeness still be single in his thirties? Yet, despite his model looks, Reece was not one to sleep around or break women's hearts. Like their late father, Reece was a principled and clear-headed man who did not fit the stereotype of Jamaicans as Caribbean Lotharios. She was grateful for him every day for this and many other things.

 How are you doing, sis?" Reece said, embracing Shanice in a tight hug that instantly lifted her spirits.

"Same old, Reece, same old," Shanice said, hearing the exhaustion in her own voice. "Still paying increasingly extortionate London rent, working long shifts all week and studying for my youth worker exams at night. Oh, and desperately trying not to lose my sanity juggling it all." The urge to cry rose in her, but Shanice pushed it down. She had been having fits of tears lately but in private. After everything Gavin had been through, Shanice couldn't let her son see her wailing. She needed to remain strong. For both of them.

"If anyone can juggle all that, it's you, sis, " Reece said, smiling warmly at her. "Remember what dad used to say about you?"

Shanice chuckled at the fond memory of their father. "They should call me Octopussy because I can do eight things simultaneously. Octopussy was his favourite James Bond film." Shanice looked away from Reece and watched as Gavin lifted the first suitcase from the boot. She let out a heavy sigh. "I wish dad was still here. I could use his silly jokes right now…and his guidance. Gavin was now taking out the second and final suitcase from the boot. "My son has been through so much for a boy his age. How I wish he did not have to go through all of this."

Reece gently placed his hands on Shanice's shoulders. She turned to face him. "I know the last months haven't been easy on Gavin or yourself. But everything's going to be ok, sis. I promise."

This time, Shanice couldn't keep the waterworks at bay. Stinging tears slid down her cheeks as she began to sob quietly. "Thank you for doing this, Reece. I know you didn't have to take this responsibility. He's not your son."

Reece wiped her tears with the palm of his left hand. "No, he's not my son but he's a Campbell. And you know what dad used to say: 'we Campbells *gwarn* look after each other, come heaven or hell'."

"…or thunder and brimstone," Shanice said, wiping the last tear from her right eye. She let out a light laugh. "God, dad was so dramatic sometimes."

"Yeah, he was."

There was a brief moment of silence as Shanice and Reece enjoyed the fond memories of their dad. Shanice broke the stillness. "I have to get going as I agreed to cover someone's Saturday shift at the restaurant today. I needed the extra money. Do you want me to help Gavin carry the suitcases inside?"

"Nah, don't worry about it, sis. Gavin's a big boy now," Reece said as he looked over Shanice's shoulder to see Gavin closing the car's boot. "He can carry his own suitcases inside. And sis, I promise you, I'll take good care of him."

Shanice smiled. "I know you will. Let me go and say goodbye to him before I go."

"I am off now," Shanice said as she came to stand in front of Gavin. He was holding two black suitcases in his hands. The frown was still across his face. "I will call you on your mobile phone every Wednesday, Friday and Sunday evening, ok. I know you wanted to stay in Brixton, but you'll make new friends here, and uncle Reece is going to take good care of you." Gavin rolled his eyes and said nothing. Shanice sighed and hugged her son, but Gavin's arms remained limp by his side.

Shanice stepped back and gave Gavin a peck on the cheek even though he did not say goodbye to her. Deciding not to force it, Shanice walked to the driver's side of the car. Before she got inside, she watched Gavin walk over to Reece, who pointed him towards the front door of Reece's flat at the end of the block. Shanice observed Gavin, still looking as if his whole world was ending, stomp towards the door. He twisted the handle and lumbered into Reece's flat, dragging both suitcases.

At that moment, Shanice was possessed by a strong urge to call her son and ask him to get back into the car. But she stopped herself. Gavin had been abandoned by his father and had now lost his childhood friend too. Gavin needed to be around a good man who could guide him through this challenging period. With everything going on in her life, Shanice felt she was currently ill-equipped to raise her son alone right now. Sending her son away was a desperate act of love, not her abandoning her responsibilities as a mother.

Forcing herself to look away from Reece's flat, Shanice got into her Ford Focus. She waved goodbye to Reece before switching on the engine with the turn of the key and drove out of the estate, making her way back to Brixton and leaving her son's care in her brother's hands.

Chapter Two
The barbershop
January 2008

The first thought that came to Gavin as soon as he stepped into uncle Reece's living room was that he was hungry.

Man, I need to munch.

Gavin dropped both suitcases right in the middle of the living room with a loud thud. He itched his scalp while observing his new environment. Uncle Reece's flat looked even smaller than the two-bedroom flat in Brixton where Gavin had lived all his life with his mum. That was until his mum further messed up his already messed-up life and moved him to Hackney.

The loud, growling sound from his stomach made Gavin look around for the kitchen. He wasted no time pacing towards it when he noticed the doorway to the kitchen a few steps away.

It was a small kitchen with a wooden table on the left and a glass bowl with some apples and oranges. A big, bright flag of Jamaica, with its green, black and yellow colours, hung from the top of the white fridge. The kitchen sink was surprisingly clean and empty, which was never the case when Gavin lived with his mum. He would always pile the sink high with plates causing his mum to moan and groan in his ears when she came back from her work shifts.

There better be some curry goat in here. Gavin eagerly opened his uncle's fridge and peered inside. Instead of finding a refrigerator filled with curry goat, rice and peas, ice cream or even milk, Gavin was greeted with the pathetic sight of a square, cardboard box with two slices of dry-looking pepperoni pizza inside. There was also a case of butter and a can of Guinness.

Gavin pulled his head out of the fridge and wondered why his uncle lived like a tramp. As he closed the fridge door, he heard someone clear their throat. Gavin turned to see his uncle standing by the doorway with his hands folded across his chest. There was a playful grin on his face.

"You've been in my house for less than five minutes, and your head is already inside my fridge," uncle Reece said.

"Yo, why is your fridge bare empty, man?" Gavin said, rubbing his demanding stomach and making his annoyance clear in his tone. "I am hungry, innit."

The smile on uncle Reece's face changed so quickly into a frown that Gavin immediately regretted being a little too casual with him.

"Let's get one thing straight," uncle Reece started, in a calm but deadly serious tone, "You don't ever address me as 'Yo' again. I am not one of your *bredrins*. You get that, nephew?

Gavin rolled his eyes and shook his head. *Already acting like his my dad or something.* This was precisely why Gavin didn't want his mum to send him to live with uncle Reece.

"Yeah, alright then," Gavin said, kissing his teeth as he looked away from his uncle.

"Alright then, what?"

A loud and impatient sigh left Gavin's mouth before he answered, "Yeah, alright then, *uncle Reece.*" Gavin placed extra emphasis on the word 'uncle.'

"Good," uncle Reece said, in a satisfying tone that instantly got on Gavin's nerves. His uncle unfolded his arms and leaned against the kitchen's doorframe. "I've been so busy today at the barbershop that I haven't had time to do shopping, so I am heading to Tesco now to buy some food. Don't worry; I will not let my nephew starve."

If uncle Reece was expecting a laugh out of Gavin, he would not get one. Gavin rolled his eyes.

"Go and pick up the suitcases you've dumped in my living room and take them to your room upstairs on the left. Do it now, please."

With a groan, Gavin dragged himself out of the kitchen and lumbered towards the two suitcases. As he picked them both up, uncle Reece walked past him towards the front door. Doing his best to ignore his protesting belly, Gavin climbed up the stairs, dragging both suitcases by his side. When he reached the landing, uncle Reece called his name. Gavin cursed under his breath. *What does he want now, man?* Gavin turned around to look at his uncle standing at the stair's landing. Car keys were clutched in his right hand.

"Now that you're living with me, Gavin, I have some house rules. No PlayStation 2 on weekdays, I want you in bed by 9pm, and whenever you eat *my* food in *my* house, you will clean up after yourself. Is that clear?"

Gavin sighed. "Yeah, man…I mean, yes, uncle Reece."

A satisfied look on his face, uncle Reece turned around, opened the front door and stepped outside, closing the front door behind him. Relieved that his uncle was finally off his case, for now anyway, Gavin dragged himself and his two suitcases into his new room.

The tiny kitchen downstairs felt like an entire living room compared to the box-sized room Gavin was standing in. To his right was a small, single bed with wooden bedframes and on the left of the room was a small, dark brown wardrobe that was barely as tall as him. At least he had a window that provided a decent view of the estate and brought some light that bounced off the ugly, green-coloured walls. Gavin was sure he would have more leg room in a prison cell.

With an exhaustive sigh, Gavin threw both suitcases onto the wooden floor, which creaked as he walked. He knelt in front of one of the suitcases, unzipped it and began taking some of his clothes out and flinging them onto the bed. Gavin only wore two brands, Nike and Adidas, and had his favourite trainers, the Nike Air Max 95s. As he rummaged through his suitcase to find them, he noticed his red and white Arsenal jersey folded neatly. It had Van Persie, his favourite player, stitched on the back.

Gavin picked up the Arsenal jersey. As he unfolded it, a card fell out of the sleeve and glided onto the floor. Gavin stared at the card for a few seconds but then carefully stretched out his right hand, which was now trembling, and picked up the card, knowing in his heart what it was.

It was a Pokémon card. Gavin had always thought that Pokémon was kind of dumb. *How could monsters that big fit in something the size of a tennis ball?* But Jamal had loved Pokémon. And Digimon, Yu-Gi-Oh and Dragonball Z, although almost every boy loved that cartoon. But Jamal had been the biggest Pokémon fan Gavin knew. Gavin stared at the orange-skinned dragon monster, Charizard, displayed on the card. Like a faint MP3 recording in his head, he heard Jamal's voice from a memory not so long ago.

"I know you think Pokemon is neeky, innit. But I am gonna give you Charizard 'cause you're bare stubborn like him."

Gavin felt the stinging in his eyes before the tears trickled down his cheeks. His chest became tighter, and he struggled to catch his breath, so he leaned back against the bed's frame. He put the Charizard Pokémon card inside the right pocket of his tracksuit and bowed his head between his knees.

He sobbed uncontrollably for a long time in that small, still bedroom. Only the sound of kids playing football outside kept him company.

******

According to his mum, it would take a week for Gavin's new school in Dalston, Kingsland Academy, to process the documents for his arrival as a new year 7 pupil.

When Gavin heard this, he was initially excited. Now he had an extra three weeks off and would use this time wisely. This meant playing season mode with Arsenal on FIFA 2007 all day and listening to the new CDs his mum had bought for him – Lethal Bizzle's *'Back to Bizznizz'* and T.I's *'T.I vs T.I.P'*.

But Gavin's plans for an extended holiday of chilling had been quickly dashed in the bin by uncle Reece. After just a single day of moving in with him, uncle Reece had given Gavin a day job as an assistant at his barbershop in Hackney, *Cutz and Trimz.*

All Gavin did at the barbershop was sweep curly fluffs of black men's hair, fetch razor clippers on demand and be ordered by his uncle to buy him chicken wings, chips and ginger beer for two pounds. Being a barber's assistant felt like cheap labour.

There were only two good things about working at the barbershop. For one, Gavin was being paid five pound a day in cash, and Gavin was saving this money to buy some new Nike Air Force 1s for summer. The other good thing was that the barbershop was located on Mare Street, a long high street close to Hackney Central station. Its location gave Gavin a good view of the school kids who went to Kingsland Academy and walked past the barbershop to hang out in front of the McDonalds down the street.

Every day, at around 5pm, Gavin would stand by the window, broom in his hand, and watch Kingsland Academy pupils, with their black blazers and black ties, walk past in groups. Like in Brixton, the school kids mostly carried small Nike backpacks, and some had flung bright yellow JD Sports bags over their shoulders. Some of the kids didn't even have any schoolbags at all. These kids, mainly the boys, would have their ties loosened around their shirt collar, slightly unbuttoned shirts, and trousers sagging low so you could see the top half of their boxers. Clearly, these were the *rude boys*. One particular black boy was always surrounded by a group of boys and girls as if he were some famous rapper. He had caught Gavin's attention immediately the first time he saw him. The boy wore a black and grey baseball cap, had two massive, glimmering studs on each ear and had silver grills attached to the bottom set of his teeth. To complete his bad boy look, he had two slits shaved into his left eyebrow. Not knowing why he felt this way, Gavin got a bad vibe about this boy.

Five days before he was due to start year 7 at his new school, Gavin saw the most beautiful girl he had ever seen in his whole life while sweeping hair at the barbershop. The girl, who looked mixed-raced, resembled a young Alicia keys with her soft and milky complexion, long, black hair which reached her shoulders and dark hazelnut eyes. Even her upper lip curved perfectly. She wore a pink bandanna which made her stand out from the other girls around her. The mysterious girl, who looked around Gavin's age but more developed than the average young teen, was walking beside the black boy with the black and grey baseball cap and grills, and he had his arms around her. Gavin felt a sharp stab of jealousy in his chest.

"Gavin! Hey, Gavin!"

Carried away by the beauty of the mysterious brown-skinned girl, Gavin had not even noticed his uncle had been calling his name repeatedly. On the third shout of his name, Gavin was pulled back to where he was. Still feeling lightheaded from seeing a girl who was so good-looking it was like she was from a rapper's music video, Gavin turned around. Uncle Reece was standing next to the reclining barber chair. It was currently occupied by a customer with a blue gown over his body covered in round hair fluffs. Half of the customer's afro was missing. Uncle Reece narrowed his eyes.

"I've been calling you for a whole minute, but you were staring out the window like you just saw the ghost of Bob Marley walk past," uncle Reece said, shaking his head at Gavin. "Anyway, I need you to go to Dixy and get me four wings and chips. And don't forget my ginger beer this time, or I'll send you right back."

******

The second week of January arrived quickly. It was the first week at Gavin's new school.

Gavin was sitting in the passenger's seat of uncle Reece's white Volkswagen Golf as he looked at Kingsland Academy's long, black school gates. Hundreds of pupils walked into the orange-coloured secondary school building or the adjacent sixth form college. Some pupils, mostly the younger ones, were being ushered in by a few teachers standing outside the gates. The constant, loud chatter of young kids and teenagers filled the air and Gavin's ears. It was nerve-racking seeing so many unrecognizable faces.

To help calm his nerves, Gavin dipped into the breast pocket inside his puffy Nike coat and retrieved the Pokémon card that Jamal had given him. Having the Pokémon card close to him made him feel less alone and anxious. Although Gavin would never admit this to anyone out loud, the Pokémon card felt like it contained Jamal's spirit within it. He would always be with Gavin as long as he had it close.

"What's that in your hand?" uncle Reece asked as he switched off the car's engine.

Gavin swiftly returned the Pokémon card to its place inside his coat. "It's nothing."

Uncle Reece eyed Gavin for a moment. "I know you're nervous, nephew," his uncle began, placing his right hand gently on Gavin's left shoulder, "it's a new school, a new area, and with new kids and new teachers. But it's a good school. Be an attentive student, work hard and don't cause trouble. And you'll be alright."

It's never that simple, Gavin thought as he listened to his uncle's basic advice. Gavin had never been in a position where he was starting a new school and didn't know anyone. Back in Brixton, most of his friends from his primary school planned on attending the same secondary school that Gavin was initially supposed to go to with Jamal. But that was never going to happen now.

"Ok, I am gonna go," Gavin said, placing his hand on the car's door handle. "Bye."

"I'll see you later," uncle Reece said, patting Gavin's back as Gavin climbed out of the car. "Remember, I want you home by 6pm and phone me if you're unsure what bus to take. Good luck, nephew."

Without looking back at his uncle, Gavin stepped outside into the noisy and chaotic crowd of school kids moving like a wave in front of him. Heart pounding, Gavin made his way to his new school.

Chapter Three

Kingsland Academy

January 2008

Growing up in Angell Town estate all his life, Gavin knew every part of Brixton like a mechanic knew every aspect of a car's engine. Anyone who loved basketball, like Jamal had, would do all they could to get a spot in Brixton Top Cats, the best basketball team in South London. If you wanted to buy some cheap headphones or a counterfeit name-brand tracksuit, you went to the market on Electric Avenue. The best chicken and chips in Brixton were Morley's.

And the dangers of Brixton, Gavin knew those too. From the hood wisdom passed down by *olders* in the area, Gavin learned what streets to avoid if he did not want to cross paths with the Peckham gangs, who had a longstanding feud with Brixton boys. He knew the guys on his estate who were not afraid to dance with bullets and roadman who carried sharp blades that drew blood and took life.

Yet Gavin knew nothing about Hackney. He felt like a rabbit in a den of foxes. If Jamal were here, he would say, *'You're slipping, bruv.'* But Gavin had no choice. Hackney was his *ends* now, and he would have to quickly adapt, the same way he had learned to navigate the streets of Brixton.

These thoughts whirled through Gavin's mind as he walked through the busy corridors of Kingsland Academy filled with chatting students. Some pupils, mostly the girls, gave him a curious glance. Yet the boys gave him a suspicious look. It was as if his unfamiliarity made him untrustworthy automatically.

A week ago, Gavin received a schedule in the post outlining his first week at his new school. Now holding the agenda in his hand, Gavin saw that he first needed to go to the headmaster's office for a brief induction.

Three girls, who looked around Gavin's age, were standing by the orange lockers and talking to each other with excitement as if some big event had just happened in their lives. They were a mixed group of girls, one white, one black and one Indian with a hijab. They looked friendly enough, so Gavin approached them to ask for directions.

"Hey girls, my name's Gavin, and I am new here," Gavin said. All three girls turned to look at him, and the white girl already had a wide grin on her freckled face. "Do you know where the headmaster's office is?"

"Hey, new boy," the white girl said, twisting a strand of her curly ginger hair as she chewed on some gum. The two other girls began to giggle. "It's on the second floor on the first corridor to your right." The girl bit her lip at Gavin, and he grinned back at her. She was definitely cute but not really his type.

"Safe," Gavin said as he turned around and walked away from the girls. He could still hear their high-pitched giggles and felt their eyes following him as he climbed up some metal stairs which led to the second floor.

The corridor where the headmaster's office was located was empty. Gavin stood in front of a black door with a golden handle. A plastic sign was attached to the door with a name written in big, bold letters:

Mrs Beatrice Churchill, Headmaster.

Gavin knocked on the door, and a voice belonging to an older woman responded.

"You can come in."

Gavin twisted the golden handle, pushed the door and walked in.

Immediately, Gavin noticed the dozens of framed pictures of students hanging from the walls in the white-painted office. The second thing that caught his attention was the black boy sitting in the chair beside the headmaster's desk. Looking no older than twelve, the boy had a dark complexion, much darker than Gavin's light brown skin tone. He had short, black hair, which Gavin could tell had recently been trimmed due to the fresh fade and the visible shape up. Although the boy had a nice haircut, Gavin noticed that his shoes looked worn out, as if he had bought them from a second-hand shop or they had been passed down. The black boy looked at Gavin and nodded his head, and Gavin did the same. He seemed oddly recognizable, but Gavin could not remember where he had seen his face before.

"Good morning, you must be Gavin Campbell," said the woman at the desk, who Gavin assumed was Mrs Churchill. Gavin nodded at his new headmaster, who wore big, round glasses just above the tip of her pointy nose. Her lips were thin, and she had tied her brunette hair into a bun. She stood up, walked around her desk towards Gavin and stretched out her hand.

"It's a pleasure to meet you, Gavin. I am Mrs Churchil, the headmaster at Kingsland Academy, and I personally wanted to welcome you on your first day." As she gave Gavin a firm handshake with a smile, Gavin could already tell that behind Mrs Churchill's friendliness was a woman whose wrong side you did not want to get on. Mrs Churchill let go of Gavin's hand.

"Here at Kingsland Academy, we understand how intimidating it can be to start a new school," Mrs Churchill started, sitting back down behind her desk.

"Since you're joining us halfway through the first term, I know it must be overwhelming for you with all the new faces. So, to help you settle in, I have assigned you a buddy who will look after you over the coming weeks." Mrs Churchill turned towards the black boy sitting on the chair and gestured towards him. "I like you to meet Yemi Abimbola. He is one of the brightest students in year 7 and will be your buddy. He will show you around the school and help you settle in."

Yemi now smiled at Gavin, and Gavin returned a smile of his own. Yemi was the first boy at this school who had actually given Gavin a friendly smile rather than *screw face* him like he was already a threat.

Mrs Churchill glanced at the clock on the wall. "You will have to do the register with your set class, which is set 7B, I believe. Yemi is in the same set as you, so he will take you to the class where you will do the register and meet your set teacher for the first time."

Yemi stood from the chair and walked towards Gavin. He nodded his head at the door for Gavin to follow him. Gavin gave Mrs Churchill a faint smile before following Yemi out of the room. Before he closed the headmaster's door, Gavin heard Mrs Churchill's voice again.

"I hope you have a good first day at Kingsland Academy, Gavin. I am sure you'll settle in without any trouble."

******

Most of the pupils had gone to their set class to take the morning register by the time Gavin and Yemi had left Mrs Churchill's office. The wide corridors were mainly empty now, but Gavin noticed a few students who lingered around the school's hallways. While walking through a corridor with Yemi, Gavin noticed two older students, a black boy and a white girl, a few years older than Gavin, kissing each other by the stairwell. The boy had his left hand up the girl's skirt.

Yemi's voice made Gavin look away from the two snogging students.

"Oi, don't you recognise me?" Yemi said. For a reason that was lost to Gavin, Yemi had a cheeky grin.

Gavin looked hard at Yemi's dark brown face. There was a familiarity to it, but Gavin's brain struggled to pinpoint exactly where he knew it from.

Noticing the mental struggle that Gavin was going through, Yemi let out a chuckle and smacked Gavin on the shoulder. "We live on the same estate, bruv. Pembury, innit. I swear you live in Crandale house as well with the guy who cuts hair?"

The recognition zapped Gavin's brain like a bolt of electricity. Yes, Gavin had seen Yemi around the estate. He often played football in the middle of the estate's enclosure with another black boy whose face Gavin could not retrieve from memory right now. "Oh yeah," Gavin said, grinning. He curled his right hand into a fist and bashed it against Yemi's raised fist. "I knew I clocked your face from somewhere. Yeah, that's my uncle, innit."

"Seen," Yemi said, nodding his head as he took a left turn into another corridor, Gavin following. "You're from south, innit?"

Gavin raised his eyebrows at Yemi. "Yeah, I am from Brixton sides. How'd you know I was from south?"

"Last week, Mrs Churchill told the whole of year 7 during our assembly that a new boy from Brixton was coming to Kingsland Academy. Everyone's been chatting about it since." Yemi must have realised the horror stretching on Gavin's face like a long shadow because he followed up with, "but it's calm, man. Everyone's mostly safe, and you're with me, innit. I am your buddy, so I got you."

As they fell into a silent walk, Gavin briefly looked at Yemi. He was slightly shorter than Gavin, but he walked with his head high and he had straight posture, even though he wore battered shoes. Even his uniform seemed scruffy now that Gavin was looking closely at him. But Yemi had natural confidence in him, which made Gavin feel a bit more relaxed.

"Are you…African?" Gavin asked.

Yemi winked at Gavin. "Yeah. My parents are from Nigeria, but I was born in Hackney, innit. You're Caribbean, yeah?"

Gavin nodded his head. "Yeah, my mum's Jamaican, innit." At his primary school in Brixton, a few kids were Nigerian, Ghanaian, Angolan and Somalian but most of the kids were from Caribbean countries. But also, Gavin had not really made friends with the kids who had African parents. Most of his friends, like Jamal, had Caribbean heritage because his mum was friends with other Caribbean parents. But maybe Yemi could be his first friend who had African heritage rather than a Jamaican one. There was a first time for everything.

******

After Gavin had read out his name during the register with Yemi and the other students in set 7B, it was time for his lessons. Luck wasn't on his side because his first lessons were English and Science, which were Gavin's most hated subjects. As the teachers talked about something called photosynthesis or rattled on about some book called *Lord Of The Flies,* which he couldn't care less about, Gavin found himself struggling to concentrate.

But at least Yemi was in his classes. When the teacher wasn't paying attention, Gavin would learn across his desk and speak to Yemi about music when they sat beside each other. It turned out Yemi was just as into Grime, Rap and R'n'B music as Gavin was. Even though he had only known him for a few hours, Gavin already felt like Yemi could be one of his best friends at this school.

By the time the one-hour lunch break arrived, Gavin had a throbbing headache from all the boring lessons he had been forced to endure, and his stomach was grumbling loudly.

With an empty blue tray in his hand, Gavin stood behind Yemi. They were queuing up in the big, noisy cafeteria, filled with chattering and hungry students, to collect their lunch. Like Gavin, Yemi was also on free school meals.

Yemi turned around to speak to Gavin. "When you've got your food, just follow me, yeah. We're gonna sit with the *mandem*."

The big black dinner lady who served the food looked like she had been born grumpy and miserable as Gavin stood in front of her and held out his tray. With a passive face, she scooped an unappealing lump of mashed potatoes onto Gavin's plate. She poured watery gravy on top of it before placing three of the saddest-looking sausages Gavin had ever seen onto his plate. Gavin squirmed at his lunch and looked up at the dinner lady, ready to protest, until he saw her nostrils flare like a dragon. Gavin decided it was best he kept his mouth shut and kept it moving.

There was so much activity in the dining hall that lunchtime seemed the most exciting part of the school day. More so than the short fifteen minute break all the students were allowed to have after their first two lessons of the school day.

Carrying his tray with its unappealing lunch, Gavin followed Yemi across the cafeteria, passing the horde of students engaged in some activity. At one dinner table, a group of black boys banged the benches with their fists, making a beat with their hands, while another boy started rapping some lyrics to the beat's rhythm. There was a mixed group of boys on another table dissing each other with 'your mum is so fat" insults. The prettiest girls, which also meant they were the most popular, were less noisy than the boys. They mostly sat in female-only groups and chatted animatedly with each other or showed their friends something on their phones.

At the corner of the cafeteria, a short black boy in a wool hat was selling Sainsbury's doughnuts and Lucozade drinks. A boy beside him opened a bag filled with poor-quality bootleg DVDs of the latest films. He also had copies of the notoriously hard-to-find 'Lord of the Mics' DVD, a legendary compilation of London's best grime MCs battling it out. Everywhere Gavin looked in the cafeteria, there was some activity going on. It felt like a busy marketplace.

Yemi led Gavin to a rectangular dining table on the other side of the dining hall. Four black boys of varying complexions were seated at the table. They all nodded their heads in acknowledgement at Yemi but gave Gavin a suspicious stare as they both sat down opposite them. By now, Gavin was used to the school boys' unfriendly looks and he started to understand why. He was the new kid in their territory. The boy sitting opposite Gavin had a big frame, and a mini afro and Gavin couldn't help but smile as the boy reminded him of Mark Henry from WWE. As Gavin studied the hugely built boy, he started to look familiar. Gavin was sure he was the other boy who played football with Yemi on the estate.

"Oi, you man, stop eating like your parents don't feed you at home for one second. I wanna introduce the new boy," Yemi said with confident authority. Immediately all four boys stopped wolfing down their bangers and mash and turned to face Gavin. "This is Gavin, innit. I am his buddy, so he's gonna be rolling with us from now on. You man got that, yeah?"

The lankiest boy, whose head humorously resembled an egg, gave Gavin a probing look. "You're the boy from south, I swear? I hear you man are proper mad down them sides. Like people get shot in those ends every day. Is it true?" The lanky boy leaned in towards Gavin.

"Allow it, man," Yemi said, rolling his eyes as he pushed the boy back. He turned to face Gavin and put his arm around him. "Sorry 'bout that, bruv. The mandem got no manners sometimes. Let me introduce you to these lot. Toby is the one who just opened his big mouth; he's Nigerian like me." Yemi then pointed at the light-skinned boy wearing a blue New York Yankees baseball cap. "That's Carlos; he's Angolan and is sick at football." Yemi's finger hovered towards the third boy, wearing a grey Adidas jacket and a grey woolly hat. "That's Andrew; he's from Jamaica like you." Gavin nodded at his fellow Jamaican, who acknowledged him with a nod back. Finally, Yemi's finger landed on the hugely built black boy who looked familiar to Gavin. "And this is my Ghanaian brother from another mother, Kwesi, but everyone calls him Big K because he's the biggest boy in year 7, you get me. My guy could easily choke slam boys in year 8 or year 9, any day of the week."

Kwesi shook his head and looked slightly embarrassed by Yemi's declaration of his mighty strength. Given Kwesi's stature, it wasn't unbelievable. Kwesi gave Gavin a big smile and extended his clenched fist towards him. "Nice to meet you, man." Gavin raised his arm and fist bumped Kwesi. Following Kwesi's lead, the other three boys bashed their clenched fists against Gavin's. The induction was complete; Gavin was now one of the *mandem*.

"Oh yeah, I forgot to mention that Big K lives in Pembury estate and in Crandale house like us," Yemi said, patting Kwesi on the shoulder. "We're the Crandale crew, dun know!"

Gavin had been right about Kwesi being from the estate and joined the boys in their collective laughter as they made fun of the group name Yemi had given them. After the laughter quietened, the boys started talking about the latest football scores. Gavin was glad that Andrew, Toby and Carlos supported Arsenal. Kwesi, much to Gavin's disappointment, supported Man United and Yemi, much to Gavin's surprise, did not watch football at all.

"You lot are too gassed over football, man," Yemi said, biting into the sausage impaled on his fork. "Music and boxing are more my ting."

As the boys, apart from Yemi, continued to debate about Man Utd and Arsenal's track record, Gavin looked around the cafeteria.

When Gavin spotted her walking across the hall with another girl by her side, his heart somersaulted in his chest. The mixed-raced beauty Gavin had been mesmerised by when he first saw her from the window of uncle Reece's barbershop looked even more dazzling up close. Her long, black hair had now been twisted into stringy curls and she wore her signature pink bandana.

His eyes still following the beautiful girl, Gavin tapped Yemi urgently on the shoulder as if Yemi had information that would save his life.

"What's up, man?"

Gavin pointed at the mixed-race girl with the pink bandanna as she sat at a cafeteria table with the other girl. "Bruv, who is that girl?"

"You mean the girl with the light brown skin and the nose piercing?" Yemi said in a tone that suggested he had been watching the other girl closely. "That's Mabel Sanchez. She's in our year."

Gavin shook his head. "Nah, not her. The girl sitting next to her, with the pink bandana?"

"Oooh, you were talking about her. That's Jamella Greenwood." Yemi grinned at Gavin as Gavin kept his eyes on her. "Yeah, bruv, she's one of the pengest tings in our year, still."

"Jamella is not just the buffest girl in year 7," Toby interjected passionately. "She's like the Barcelona of girls in our whole school. She's champions league, and every other girl is basically division one."

Kwesi, the only one in the group to have devoured his entire lunch, chimed in. "I hear she's linking Nasher in year 9 though. So if I was you, I wouldn't even try to move to her. Everyone will soon tell you that Nasher is a crazy guy. You don't wanna be chatting to his girl, innit."

But Gavin had barely registered Kwesi's warning. *So that's her name. Jamella Greenwood.* Somehow Gavin would have to speak to her. He just had to.

Yemi winked at Gavin and elbowed him lightly in the rib. "Don't get too excited, but she's gonna be in our drama lesson right after lunch."

Chapter Four

She's feeling you

January 2008

Miss Aldridge, Gavin's drama teacher, looked like one of those psychics who tried to predict your future while holding a crystal ball in front of you. She had pink dyed hair, wore two giant butterfly-shaped earrings and had big, round spectacles. She was currently trying to gain some control over her chattering and energetic pupils.

Sitting cross-legged on a soft mat, Gavin was in a semi-circle with fifteen other year 7 students. Yemi and Kwesi sat together beside him. Gavin scanned the room to try and find Jamella, but he could not see her. Maybe she was just going to be late.

"Can everyone please quieten down," Miss Aldridge said, sitting in a plastic chair as she faced her students. She was doing her best to raise her squeaky voice to its loudest but failed to break past the chorus of noise coming from her pupils. "Please, everyone, I need to start the lesson. Shequan, please stop trying to poke Ahmed's eye with a pencil."

After ten minutes, Miss Aldridge finally managed to calm the class down. Gavin looked around again and noticed Jamella was still not in the room. His heart sank with disappointment.

Once every student was quiet, Miss Aldridge picked up a plastic board with a sheet of paper listing every pupil's name and began to call the register.

"Matilda?"

"Here."

"Abdul?"

"Here."

"Tinuke?"

"Here."

"Jamella?"

There was no response. Miss Aldridge called Jamella's name again. The classroom door swung open, and everyone turned their attention to the two girls who had entered the room. Jamella, who had taken off her pink bandanna, walked through the door with Mabel by her side. She was giggling to Mabel as she shut the door behind her.

Miss Aldridge scowled at the two girls. "Jamella and Mabel. You're fifteen minutes late to class."

Jamella looked genuinely remorseful when told this, but Mabel gave Miss Aldridge a dirty look and kissed her teeth loudly. Both girls joined the semicircle.

"Sorry, Miss Aldridge," Jamella said. Gavin swooned over her voice. He didn't expect her to have such a strong, Caribbean accent. It sounded like she was from Barbados as the tone and rhythm of her accent were similar to Rihanna's, the pop singer. Jamella could not have been born in London with an accent like that.

Once the register was complete, Miss Aldridge put the board on a nearby table. She then took a binding booklet from behind her and presented it to the class as if she was showing off a rare diamond. There was no title on the cover. "Can anyone tell me what play this is? I did mention it last week."

Gavin looked at Yemi and Kwesi, who both shrugged their shoulders. Most of the students looked bored of the lesson already. Glancing at Jamella, Gavin saw her giggle as Mabel whispered something in her ear. Finally, one student, a lanky Indian boy with a thin face and big ears, saved the class from the awkward stretch of silence.

"Is it Romeo and Juliet?" the lanky Indian boy said.

The way Miss Aldridge's face lit up, Gavin would have thought someone had just asked to marry her.

"That's correct, Imran. Well done. Today, we're going to act out one of the first scenes in the play where Romeo and Juliet meet. Any volunteers?"

Gavin chuckled as everyone in the class avoided Miss Aldridge's desperate eyes. Kwesi leaned forward and pointed at Yemi.

"Bruv, why are you pointing at me?" Yemi said, slapping Kwesi's hand away as Gavin laughed at their banter. "You should volunteer to be Juliet."

"Looks like everyone is too excited to volunteer," Miss Aldridge said, her sarcasm failing to hide the disappointment in her voice. "Very well, I shall have to pick two people." Miss Aldridge's eyes scanned the room as the students either looked away or bowed their heads, avoiding her laser-focused eyes. The drama teacher pointed her finger directly at Jamella. "Since you were late, you can be Juliet today, Jamella. Please come to the front of the class."

Jamella looked around the class. Some of the students had now started to snicker. Jamella stood up and walked to the front.

Gavin almost fell backwards, as if Miss Aldridge had zapped him with electricity from her finger when she pointed at him. "And you're the new student, yes? Gavin Campbell, is it?"

Swallowing some salvia and feeling his armpits go moist, Gavin nodded his head sheepishly.

"Excellent. Today Gavin, I would like you to act out the part of Romeo. Please come to the front of the class."

Gavin did not consider himself shy, but right now, he felt like he wasn't wearing any boxers as he made his way to the front of the class with his head down. *Come on, bruv, don't look scared in front of her.* When Gavin got to the front, he raised his head to look at Jamella, his heart pounding in his chest like a drum. Much to his surprise, Jamella was smiling at him. She pushed back her curly, dark hair and straightened her skirt. At that moment, standing in her presence, Gavin was breathless. How could God create a girl so good looking?

Miss Aldridge handed Gavin and Jamella each a copy of Shakespeare's play as the class waited in eager silence. " Please turn to act one, scene five. And when you read your respective parts, try putting yourselves in the character's minds. Both Romeo and Juliet are instantly attracted to each other. This is love at first sight, remember. So let that shine through as you read."

Gavin was not into this acting stuff. He liked to watch football and listen to rap music. But Jamella was staring at him now with those dark brown eyes and gave him an encouraging nod. Now feeling a strong urge to impress her, Gavin cleared his throat and began to read Romeo's dialogue.

"If I profane with my unworthiest hand. This holy shrine, the gentle sin, is this. My lips, two brushing pilgrims, ready to stand." Gavin paused briefly to study the room. The whole class and Miss Aldridge were actually buying his acting even though he did not have the foggiest idea of what he was saying.

Jamella was looking at him, but Gavin couldn't read her expression. He read the last line: "To smooth that rough touch with a tender kiss."

As soon as Gavin had finished his part, Jamella sprung to life. She spoke her lines passionately, the words dancing from her tongue with a tropical rhythm. "Good pilgrim, you do wrong your hand so much," she said, looking up at Gavin quickly and giving him a smile before looking down at her lines again. "Which mannerly devotion shows in this, for saints have hands that pilgrims' hands do touch, and palm to palm is holy palmer's kiss."

They were both getting into the spirit of the scene now. Gavin continued to read his lines, matching Jamella's enthusiasm and energy. It was effortless bouncing off her. When he looked up at her occasionally, she would either smile or stare at him like she was not just reading the play but reading him too. Gavin looked at the final line on the page. He could feel his heartbeat race when he realised the scene instructed Romeo to kiss Juliet after his last line.

Gavin stepped closer towards Jamella so they were inches apart. He could feel everyone's eyes on him as the class waited, holding their breaths, for the moment they all knew was coming. Mastering his nerves, Gavin reached out his hand and took Jamella's left hand into his own. She fluttered her eyelashes at him and bit her lip.

"Then move not, while my prayer's effect I take. Thus from my lips, by thine, my sin is plunged." Gavin gently caressed Jamella's hand; it was soft and smooth, and he raised the back of her hand to his lips.

The whole class erupted into laughter and loud whistles as soon as Gavin kissed Jamella's hand.

"Ok, everyone, please calm down," Miss Aldridge shouted over the cacophony of noise from the students. After three minutes, the delirium settled, and the year 7s quietened. "Thank you for that, Gavin and Jamella. You both played the roles of Romeo and Juliet believably. You have a natural chemistry together."

Someone in the class whistled again, and everyone howled with laughter once more. Miss Aldridge spent another minute calming the class down. "You can return to the circle, and I will pick two more people to act out the scene. Well done to the two of you for setting the bar very high."

"You were really good," Jamella said as she walked with Gavin back to the circle of students. She looked Gavin in the eye and gave him a warm smile.

"Yeah, so was you," Gavin said, grinning at her. "Our chemistry was on point, innit."

Jamella let out a short laugh which made Gavin feel dizzy with pleasure. He could listen to her laughter in his sleep.

Gavin returned to sit next to Yemi and Kwesi. Jamella went to sit next to Mabel. Throughout the rest of the class, Gavin and Jamella stole glances at each other. They would both smile when their eyes locked and then look away quickly.

Gavin felt like he was flying over the clouds. Jamella was definitely feeling him.

******

Much to Gavin's surprise, he actually felt disappointed when his first day at school was over. Even though most of the boys at Kingsland Academy had given him bad looks, at least the girls were friendly, and he had quickly found a group of boys to chill with. And then there was Jamella Greenwood. No matter how boring school lessons were, he would always come back just to see her.

It was 4pm. Gavin was standing by the metal, black railings of the school gates with Yemi, Kwesi, Andrew, Toby and Carlos. Hundreds of noisy students poured out of the school and onto the street. Some pupils, mostly the year 7s and year 8s, were whisked away by their parents. The older students in year 9 and above played football in the playground. Others were leaning on the gates to chat up the passing girls or chasing them playfully around the street, slapping their bums with their school ties. The boys who did this would ignore the shouts of the school teachers who stood outside the school, demanding them to stop. The sixth-form students, who wore casual clothing instead of a school uniform and mostly just stood around chatting, looked like grown adults to Gavin. Some of the sixth-form boys were already growing full beards.

"Yo, what are you man saying then?" Andrew said, who had unbuttoned his school tie and tied it around his head like he was Rambo. "Are we gonna play footy at Hackney Downs park? A couple of the mandem in our year are playing eleven-a-side, and they need more players, innit."

Yemi shrugged his shoulders. "Yeah, I'll back it. What about you, Gavin? Might as well come and meet some of the other boys from the other schools around the area. We're all safe with each other."

Gavin had been hoping to catch another glimpse of Jamella but could not see her anywhere. He let out a disappointed sigh and turned to look at Yemi. He nodded his head. "Yeah, I am down for kicking ball. I don't know where Hackney Downs park is, though."

Kwesi smacked Gavin lightly on the back. "Don't worry, man. Just follow us. It's where a lot of people go after school to chill. It's the spot."

As the boys were about to head off, Gavin's heart did a backflip in his chest when he saw Jamella walking directly to the group. Mabel was behind her and seemed to be pushing a reluctant Jamella towards Gavin and the rest of the boys.

"Just go and speak to him," Gavin heard Mabel mutter as she forcefully shoved her friend in front of Gavin and the other boys.

All six boys were now staring at Jamella as she stood before them. She had her hands crossed over her skirt and looked uncomfortable. Gavin looked at her, feeling his armpits go sweaty again. Mabel's eyes were on him, and it felt like it was just the two of them standing there as they stared at each other.

"Hey, it's Gavin, right?" Mabel said in a timid way that was entirely different from the confident acting she had displayed in the drama lesson earlier.

"Yeah, that's me. I mean, my name is Gavin, innit. My mum named me that name." Gavin wished he could slap himself at that moment as he heard the boys chuckle beside him. *Bruv, why would I say that?*

"Yeah, it's a nice name. I mean, it suits you a lot," Mabel said, now twisting a strand of her curly hair and biting her lip.

From behind Jamella, Mabel flung her arms in the air and huffed. "Gurl, are you serious?" she said, with both hands now by her hips. Mabel flung her attention onto Gavin, and he was taken aback by the fierceness in her eyes. She was definitely a London girl.

"Listen, Gavin, mate, Jamella wants you to hang out with us at Hackney Marshes." Mabel then looked at Yemi, and her intense expression softened. "And you can chill with us too, Yemi."

"Oh, me? Swear down?" Yemi said, pointing to himself and looking both shocked and elated. "Yeah, I am down for chilling with you girls."

"Good," Mabel said with a satisfied tone. "Follow us to Dixy to get some munch, then we'll all go together."

"Oh, so you're both not coming to football then?" Kwesi said. The disappointment in his voice did not go unnoticed.

Gavin and Yemi had already started walking off with the two girls, but Yemi turned back to look at a disheartened Kwesi. "Nah, I'll see you back at the estate, fam. And I'll see the rest of you lot tomorrow."

"Ok…have fun, I guess," Kwesi said.

******

After each buying a box of four wings, chips and coke from Dixy Chicken, Gavin, Yemi, Jamella and Mabel took the bus 276 from Shacklewell Lane to Kingsmead estate. They then jumped off the bus and made the short walk to Hackney Marshes.

Hackney Marshes was unlike anything Gavin had ever seen living in London. But to be honest, he had never really ventured outside of Brixton much growing up. Hackney Marshes was a wide grassy field that must have been the size of at least three football pitches as the open, grassy land seemed to stretch without any end. If not for the high-rise tower blocks looming in the distance, Gavin would not think he was in London anymore but in some countryside. The closest thing to Hackney Marshes in Brixton was Brockwell Park. As Gavin walked silently next to Jamella, with Yemi walking behind them with Mabel, he looked around the grassy expanse while eating a chicken wing. As he breathed in the fresh air, Gavin realised he liked this part of Hackney and could see himself coming here a lot.

The air had become chillier as the evening began to introduce itself. Jamella, who had not brought a coat with her, began to shiver. Gavin noticed that Yemi and Mabel, who were strolling some distance behind them, had started conversating, so Gavin knew he needed to make some convo with Jamella real quick.

"You can wear my jacket if you want?"

Jamella smiled shyly at Gavin and nodded her head. Gavin removed his bag from his back, took off his puffy, black Nike jacket and put it around her. "Thanks for that. You're sweet," Jamella said, fluttering her eyelashes. Gavin loved it when she did that.

"So why did you move from Brixton to Hackney?" Mabel asked as Gavin put both his hands in his trouser pockets.

Gavin was about to mention what happened with Jamal but stopped himself. He did not want to think about all of that at this moment. "I'll tell you another time, innit." He looked at Jamella, who was at least four inches shorter than him, and wanted to pull her close to him but decided now was not the right moment. Instead, he steered the conversation in a more playful direction. "Your accent is sexy, you know that, right?"

That chat-up line had done the trick, and Jamella giggled. She edged a little closer to Gavin as they continued to walk through the grassy pathway. "You're actually funny. I grew up in Barbados up until I was ten. I have only been in London for two years, so I still have my accent. I came here to live with my auntie in Homerton."

"Oh, seen. So do you like London then? I know the weather is pretty crap."

Jamella chuckled. "Yeah, I do miss the sun and beach life of Barbados. But apart from the crap weather like you said, London is not too bad."

"So what's your favourite thing about London then?"

Jamella turned to him. She had a mischievous look as if she had thought of something naughty. "The boys are cute." Even as she said it, her eyes stayed on Gavin.

"Oh, is it? So am I one of the cute boys, then?"

Jamella giggled, and her eyes were still locked onto Gavin. "Maybe."

Emboldened, Gavin was about to lean in for a kiss until he heard the sound of a text message from his iPhone. Gavin took his brand new smartphone, which his Mum had brought him for Christmas, out of his pocket. As he expected, the text message was from uncle Reece.

It's almost 6pm. I want you home in the next 20 minutes.

Jamella must have read the annoyed expression on Gavin's face as he put the phone back in his pocket. "Is everything ok?"

"Yeah," Gavin said with a sigh, knowing he had missed his opportunity to go in for the kiss. "My uncle, who I live with, wants me back home, innit."

"Yeah, it's getting dark. Me and Mabel are gonna head home now too. Take my number. Have you got Facebook?"

"Yeah, I do. I can send you a friend request."

After exchanging numbers with the girls and promising to add them on Facebook, Gavin and Yemi left Mabel and Jamella. They took a different bus since they lived in another part of the borough. Feeling good about the evening, Gavin followed Yemi to a place called Lower Clapton, where they took the bus 38 back to Pembury estate.

The top deck of the bus was mostly empty, apart from an older woman reading a book and a roughly dressed Chinese man who was snoring and stunk of alcohol. Gavin and Yemi made their way to the back of the double-decker bus, sat down and immediately began discussing the girls.

"I can't believe on your first day at school you get the *lengest* girl in our year's number," Yemi said, fist-bumping Gavin. "You gotta teach me your bars, bruv. I am trying to be like you out here."

Gavin laughed. "Yo, real talks, I am surprised myself. I think she's proper feeling man, you know."

Yemi nodded his head. "Definitely, bruv."

"What about you and Mabel? She's got bare attitude but it's kinda attractive, I can't lie."

Yemi chuckled. "I know she acts like a hood girl, but she has a proper soft side. But I don't know if she likes me like that, you get me. I was just your wingman."

They laughed and continued talking about the two girls until the bus reached the estate. The sky was pitch black when Gavin and Yemi alighted the bus. As they walked through Crandale street to get back to their part of their estate, Gavin noticed a group of five boys, looking much older than himself and Gavin, posted by the black railings. They were a mixed group with three black boys, one Indian boy and a white boy. One of the black boys, wearing a black and grey Adidas jacket with a white New Era hat, was rapping over a grime beat playing from one of the other boy's phones. When Gavin and Yemi came closer, the boy who was rapping immediately stopped as did the music. His eyes rested on Gavin, and he narrowed them. It was not a friendly stare, and Gavin suddenly felt nervous.

The New Era hat boy stepped away from the railings and stood in the middle of the pavement, blocking Yemi and Gavin's path. The boy in the hat kept his eyes on Gavin even as he addressed Yemi. Doing his best not to appear scared, Gavin tried not to look down at the ground.

"What's good, Yemi?" How's your big sister? I don't see her around the ends anymore," the boy said, never removing his eyes from Gavin. "She was the *choongest* girl on the block."

Yemi chuckled. "Scrappy, my sister's at uni now," Yemi said, shrugging his shoulders. "Didn't she tell you?"

"I must have forgotten, innit," Scrappy said. He nodded at Gavin. "So, who's your new friend? I ain't clocked his face down these sides before?"

"This is Gavin," Yemi said in a cheerful tone. Yemi was not intimidated by Scrappy or the others on the railings, who had now turned their attention to Gavin. From their casual interaction with Yemi, Gavin figured that the boys also lived on the estate.

"Seen. So what ends you from, Gavin?" Scrappy said in an oddly aggressive voice.

"I am from Brixton," Gavin said, keeping his tone even and ensuring he did not come across as too timid. Scrappy had a dangerous aura about him.

"So, if you're from Brixton, what are you doing down my ends?"

"I am living with my uncle Reece now in…."

"Hold up," Scrappy interrupted. His face had now lit up, and his threatening glare towards Gavin vanished utterly, replaced by one of delight. "Oh…

your Reece's nephew. Say no more. Come spud man, innit." Scrappy stuck out a clenched fist.

Although he was confused about Scrappy's sudden change in his attitude towards him, Gavin was not about to reject Scrappy's gesture of friendliness. He bashed his right fist against Scrappy's.

"Your uncle is a Hackney OG, do you know that? He's got mad stories to tell about the ends. He knew some real badman in the hood," Scrappy said in an awestruck voice as if Gavin's uncle was a Hollywood celebrity. "Real talks, your uncle is one of the realest guys. He cuts my hair, innit, and told me his nephew would be living with him. Oi, listen, you roll safe round 'ere, yeah. Hackney can be rough; you get me."

Surprised to meet someone so enamoured with his uncle, who was just a boring barber to Gavin, he nodded at Scrappy, unsure what else to say. The rest of the boys leaning on the railings had become disinterested in Gavin and were checking their phones. Scrappy stepped aside, and Gavin and

Yemi continued to walk through the street before taking a left turn into a path that led to the section of the estate where Crandale house was.

"My uncle's yard is this way, innit," Gavin said, standing in front of Yemi once they were inside the enclosure of their part of the sprawling estate.

"Calm" Yemi said, fist-bumping Gavin. "I got your number now. I'll send you a friend request on Facebook. See you at school tomorrow. Safe."

Gavin waved goodbye to Yemi and headed to uncle Reece's flat. He took the key from inside his coat and unlocked the door. As Gavin entered the flat, he closed the door and walked into the living room.

Uncle Reece was sitting on the couch, with a plate of pepperpot stew on a small, wooden table in front of him. When he noticed Gavin standing by the doorway, uncle Reece turned away from watching the football game on the television.

"So, nephew," uncle Reece said, looking closely at Gavin, "how was your first day at school?"

Gavin smiled. The thought of seeing Jamella again and hanging out with Yemi and the other boys tomorrow already made him excited. "It was actually a good first day, uncle Reece. You know what, I might just like it here in Hackney."

Chapter Five

I am not that guy you want beef with

January 2008

Respect.

No matter what, you always had to have respect in the ends.

Nasher lived by this. It was a lesson that had literally been beaten into him by the fists of his two older brothers, the notorious Nash twins of London Fields estate.

And what was the best way to gain respect?

Through fear.

It was why no one who lived in Hackney, apart from his two older brothers, ever called him by his government name, Nelson Ogbodo. If you were stupid enough to do that, you would find a shank two inches from your throat.

"Oi, bruv. Your mum is so fat when she jumped into a swimming pool; she caused a tsunami."

Nasher almost spat out pieces of his Big Mac when he heard K Dot's funny diss as he sat in the

McDonald's on Mare street with his squad. There was K Dot, a scrawny Bengali boy who always made Nasher laugh with his sense of humour. Sitting beside him on the table was Harris, a short black boy who always wore a grey puffer jacket, even when the weather was boiling. He had a permanent screw face and rarely smiled. Sitting in front of him and currently engaged in a dissing contest with K Dot was Skilla, a white boy whose older brother sold guns to a few gangsters in the borough. Lastly, there was Nina, a light-skinned girl with two nose piercings, a skin fade, and a shape-up. Some people mistook Nina for a boy, but with good reason, as there was nothing girly about her. Even all of her friends were guys. She was sitting on an adjacent table with her legs stretched out so people who wanted to pass would probably have to find another way around. Nina was a proper Hackney girl who was active on the streets. Even some of the rude boys in the ends thought twice before chatting to her. She was not someone you wanted to ask to move their legs out the way, no matter how politely you asked.

Skilla kissed his teeth. "That's whack, bruv. Oi, hear this one. Your mum is so ugly that her birth certificate is a letter of apology."

"Nahhhh, that one there is a violation, you know. Bare rude," Nina said, making a loud pop with the bubble gum she was chewing. She turned her head to address Nasher. "Oi, you killed it today in the studio. Bars were fire, fam."

"Safe," Nasher said, throwing the empty Big Mac box on the floor. "Man's gonna be on radio soon. Don't watch that."

"Only a matter of time, bruv," said Harris.

All of them were still in their Kingsland Academy school uniform. They had all snuck out of school around lunchtime to go to the recording studio in Dalston. Nasher loved spitting bars to 140 bpm beats, and his squad provided the hype. If he was not beefing or robbing someone, Nasher loved music and aspired to be an MC like his favourite MCs, Kano and Ghetts, east London legends.

Nasher licked the silver grills he had fitted into his mouth, ensuring no food got stuck inside. He looked around McDonald's. It was getting busier with students from Kingsland Academy and other nearby schools in this part of Hackney. A thought occurred to Nasher when he realised he hadn't seen someone for a while.

"Oi, where's Jamella at?" Nasher said, massaging his knuckles. "Man's been chatting to her on Facebook for two weeks, and she keeps saying she's busy. You lot know what's going on with her?"

"I dunno. She's your link, bro," K Dot said, picking up some fries from inside the brown McDonald's paper bag in front of him.

Nasher flung his right hand at K Dot, knocking the fries from K Dot's fingers. He narrowed his eyes at K Dot. "Get mouthy again, and I'll backhand you like I am your Dad." K Dot lowered his eyes to the floor as the rest of the group chuckled.

Nina sat up from the bench and looked at Nasher. "Fam, I've been seeing her leave school with one light-skinned yout' with braids. I think he's new, innit. One of my youngers told me his name was Gavin when I asked her. He's in year 7."

Harris nodded his head. "Yeah, I heard about this yout'. Apparently, he's from south. Brixton sides." Harris tutted. "This guy comes to our ends, our school, and starts chatting up your girl. Are you really having that, bruv?"

"You know I ain't," Nasher said, punching his fists against the palm of his hand. "His name is Gavin, yeah? Say less. Looks I need to have a word with this yout' and let him know this ain't south London. This is Hackney, *my ends*, and he's gotta show respect, you get me."

******

"It sounds like you're enjoying your new school and making some friends."

Gavin's mum was on the loudspeaker. While speaking to her, Gavin was sitting in front of the wooden table desk in the small room he had been sleeping in for the past two weeks at uncle Reece's flat. His laptop, a stack of books from school and his iPhone were on the table. Gavin was supposed to be doing his science homework, he needed to write a short essay on five periodic table elements, but it gave him a migraine. Instead, he watched YouTube videos about Van Persie's best goals for Arsenal last season.

"Yeah, school's been alright," Gavin said, clicking on another video showcasing Van Persie's top ten moments. "Could be worse, innit."

But Gavin was deliberately being modest. He did not want to give his mum the satisfaction of knowing that maybe moving him out of Brixton to live in Hackney had not been such a bad idea.

Gavin had been attending Kingsland Academy for two weeks. He quickly found his crew with Yemi, Kwesi and the other boys. They would talk about rap and grime music every lunchtime and after school, if they were not playing football at the park. They had recently debated which MCs had gone the hardest on Lethal Bizzle's massive 2004 grime track, *'POW!'*, coming to no consensus, and discussed Arsenal's rise to the Premier League's top spot. As Gavin thought about his new school, he glanced at the Charizard Pokémon card he had placed next to the laptop and smiled. If Jamal was still here, he knew he would have liked Gavin's new friends, especially Yemi, who Gavin was beginning to see as his new best friend.

But the best thing about moving to Hackney was meeting Jamella. She was unlike any girl Gavin had ever met, and he fancied her. Hard. Ever since their walk at Hackney Marshes, they had gotten closer. If they were not texting each other at school, they were talking on Facebook. Gavin knew he would kiss her soon, but it had to be at the right moment; he couldn't mess it up.

"Well, I am so happy to hear you're settling well. Keep out of trouble, and don't stress your uncle too much."

Gavin rolled his eyes. "I won't, mum.

"Good. Well, I have to go. I have an evening class in thirty minutes. Speak soon. Love you."

"Yeah, love you too. Bye, mum."

As soon as the phone call ended, someone opened Gavin's door. He turned from his chair to see uncle Reece standing by the door, dressed in jeans and a plain, white vest. He glanced at the laptop and textbooks on the desk and gave Gavin a probing look.

"I hope you're doing some homework and not just watching football videos on the internet," uncle Reece said.

"I am doing my homework, uncle Reece," Gavin said, stopping himself from rolling his eyes.

"Ok, good. Remember to be in bed by 9pm."

Just as uncle Reece turned around to leave the room, a thought entered Gavin's head, and he suddenly wanted his uncle's advice on an issue that had been on his mind. "Hey, uncle Reece, don't leave yet. Can I ask you something?"

Uncle Reece turned back into the room and looked at Gavin expectantly. "Yes, nephew. What do you want to ask me?"

Now that he had his uncle's attention, Gavin was unsure how to actually phrase the question he wanted to ask. Seeing as uncle Reece began to tap his feet and look at him with an impatient stare, he decided to be just blunt.

"How do you know the right time to kiss a girl?"

Uncle Reece's eyes widened in shock, and Gavin smirked since he could tell his uncle was not expecting that question. "So there's a girl you fancy at school then?"

Gavin frowned. "I didn't say that."

"Ok then, if you say so," uncle Reece said, with a light chuckle, although Gavin failed to see what was funny unless he was missing something. "All I am gonna say is always make sure the girl is comfortable and read her body language; then you'll know when the right time is."

Gavin scratched his braids and thought about what his uncle had said. His uncle's answer had just created more questions. Like how were you supposed to read someone's body language? How did you know when a girl is comfortable? What were the signs? Before Gavin could ask further questions, uncle Reece spoke.

"That's enough questions about girls, nephew," uncle Reece said, his patience waning. "You need to be more concerned with your homework and less concerned about how to kiss girls. Now focus and don't watch any more football videos. I am not stupid."

Gavin groaned and turned on his chair to face his headache-inducing homework while uncle Reece closed his bedroom door.

******

The next day, Gavin lined up with Kwesi, Andrew, Toby and Carlos at the cafeteria. It was lunchtime. Hundreds of voices flying from the mouths of chattering students collided in the air, making the dinner hall reverberate like a concert arena.

Gavin looked around. "Yo, where's Yemi at? We were in maths class together, then he just dipped afterwards without telling me."

Kwesi, standing in front of Gavin with an empty tray, turned around to look at Gavin. "On my way here, I saw him chatting to some year 9 boys in the science corridor."

Gavin raised his eyebrows. "Why would Yemi be chatting to year 9s?"

Kwesi shrugged his shoulders. "Dunno. We'll ask him when he comes, innit."

Today's lunch menu was just as miserable as Gavin had expected. The dinner lady had served him soggy chips and battered cod, hard like stale bread, when Gavin poked it with his fork and squishy peas. After collecting their lunch, Gavin, Kwesi, Andrew, Toby, and Carlos sat at their usual cafeteria table, holding their lunch trays. They began discussing the latest football results in the Premier League.

"Come on, bruv, Arsenal are winning the league this year," Andrew said, throwing a piece of chips into his mouth. "We're first place in the league. Wenger is a boss. What do you have to say about that, Big K?"

Kwesi waved his right hand dismissively at Andrew. He swallowed three pieces of chips simultaneously, making Gavin chuckle before he answered. "Tottenham took you lot for dickheads in the league cup. 5-1. I know you man were all crying yourselves to sleep yesterday."

"Whatever," Gavin said, shrugging his shoulders as he joined the conversation, ready to defend Arsenal. "At the end of the day, Arsenal is still at the top of the league right now, you get me."

"Anything can change, man. It's football. One minute you're on top, and the next, you're not. All it takes is one bad match, you get me."

Before Gavin could continue defending Arsenal with all his heart, Yemi entered their vicinity, but he did not sit down. He stood in front of the table. Gavin and the rest of the boys looked at him. Yemi seemed very concerned as if something or someone had been troubling him.

"What's up, Yemz?" Gavin said, realising he was calling him 'Yemz' for the first time, but it felt natural. "Everything bless?"

Yemi nodded slowly and looked at Gavin without addressing the rest of the group. "Yeah, I am good. Gavin, bruv, Nasher wants to speak to you, innit."

Gavin looked at the boys and then back at Yemi. "Who's that?"

"He's one boy in year 9," Kwesi answered, who was now looking seriously at Yemi. "I told you before he was the guy that people were saying was doing a ting with Jamella." Kwesi shook his head. "It's never good if that guy wants to chat to you. He's a mad guy like his two older brothers."

"Nah, it's probably nothing, " Yemi said in a shaky voice. "But he wants to talk to you at the back of the school and asked me to bring you to him. So let's chat to him, see what he wants and then cut, yeah?"

Although this all sounded dodgy to Gavin, he was not going to show fear in front of the boys. Whoever this Nasher was, Gavin would not be scared of him, especially not after everything Gavin had been through with what happened to Jamal. He stood up from the cafeteria table and nodded his head at Yemi.

"Alright, come, let's go."

******

From the first day Gavin had met Yemi at the headmaster's office, Yemi seemed to have an unlimited supply of confidence. Gavin had only seen Yemi be a little timid when he was around Mabel, who he obviously fancied. But as Gavin walked beside Yemi through the mostly empty playground, there were still a few people playing football on the grass field; he saw a different side to his new friend. Yemi looked anxious, putting Gavin on edge.

After traversing the whole length of the playground, Gavin and Yemi walked down the slope of a hill. They turned a corner at the edge of the school's main building, which took them to a secluded area at the back of the school.

Gavin immediately recognised the boy leaning against the wall. He was the boy Gavin had seen from the window of uncle Reece's barbershop with the black and grey, New Era baseball cap, which he was wearing now, and grills in his teeth. The day Gavin had first seen this boy, he had his arm around Jamella.

Also leaning against the wall were five other people. Gavin noticed one of them was a girl with two nose piercings and short, shaven hair that you would typically find on a boy. She winked at Gavin and gave him a sinister grin.

The boy with the black and grey baseball cap removed himself from the wall and faced Gavin and Yemi. "Good work, my younger, bringing this yout' to me," he said, talking to Yemi directly, "you can go away now, innit."

Yemi stepped forward. "Come on, Nasher. Why do I need to leave, man?"

The girl with the two nose piercings stepped away from the wall, marched towards Yemi and gave him a light headbutt which took Gavin by surprise.

"Who are you chatting back to, bruv?" the girl said, in a rough London accent that would intimidate even grown men. "Do you year 7s have wax in your ears or something? My man said bounce, innit. So bounce before I bounce you out of here like a basketball, you get me. Dickhead."

Yemi looked at Nasher, who remained stony-faced and silent. He then turned to Gavin and gave him a silent nod which suggested that Gavin would be ok. But it did not look that way. Despite the threats from this girl, Gavin had thought Yemi would still stand his ground. Instead, Yemi turned around and plodded off in the opposite direction. Gavin looked back to see Yemi enter the school building, closing the door behind him. *How could Yemi just leave me with these lot?*

"Why are you standing there bare shook, bruv?" Nasher said, flashing his grills as he spoke. "Come over, innit. I just wanna have a chat with you."

Gavin did not like the situation he was in, but running away would not do him any good. Seeing no other choice, Gavin ambled towards Nasher. The girl with the two nose piercings walked back to the wall to join the gang.

Nasher put his arms around Gavin as he came to stand next to him. "Man's heard a lot about you, bruv", he said, his warm breath engulfing Gavin's face. "Brixton boy, yeah?" Nasher chuckled lightly. "But hear what I am saying, you ain't in south anymore, you get me. This is east London and you gotta show proper respect to the top boys round 'ere. You get what man's saying?"

Gavin wanted to slap Nasher's mouth so hard that his fake grills would fly out. As he was outnumbered, Gavin did the intelligent thing instead and nodded. "Whatever you say, innit," Gavin replied, sprinkling some defiance in his tone. He was no dickhead.

Nasher rolled his head back with laughter, and the others joined in. "This *likkle boy* giving me some attitude, you know," Nasher said with a mocking and playful tone. "He must think he's chatting to some wasteman."

Nasher was too quick, giving Gavin no time to counter. Grabbing Gavin by his school shirt, Nasher swung Gavin onto the concrete wall. Gavin let out a shriek of pain as his back slammed against the cold, brick surface. As he struggled to escape Nasher's grip, two of Nasher's goons, the girl and a white boy, grabbed each of his arms and forcibly held them. Gavin was pinned against the wall. There was no way out for him now.

Bouncing on the spot with glee on his face, as if he had just been given a prize, Nasher searched Gavin's right pocket. He took Gavin's wallet and threw it to a big black boy wearing a grey puffer jacket who caught it.

"Allow it, man," Gavin said, wiggling in desperation to escape from the clutches of the girl and the skinny white boy.

"Shut your mout'!" Nasher said, spit spraying from his mouth and landing on Gavin's face. He gave Gavin a hard slap across his right cheek. The slap stung so much that tears almost came from Gavin's eyes. "Where's all that base in your voice now? Wasteman." Nasher kissed his teeth. "Oi Harris, how much does he have in his wallet?"

Gavin turned his head and saw the boy wearing the puffer jacket take out the twenty-pound note uncle Reece had given Gavin as his weekly allowance. "Fam, we can get ourselves a big KFC bucket meal with this," Harris said. He waved the twenty-pound note in front of Gavin. There was a big smirk stretched across Harris' face.

"That's an excellent idea," Nasher said, continuing to search Gavin's pockets. He took out Gavin's iPhone. He inspected the smartphone, looking at both sides of the phone, then glared at Gavin. "Let me tell you what happens next, my younger. You're gonna delete Jamella's number from your phone. If she texts you, you don't reply back. If she tries to chat to you at school, you air her. She's my ting. And if you keep linking her, then it's gonna get long for you. I ain't the guy you want beef with, innit."

The girl with the two nose piercings and the white boy let go of Gavin's arms. Gavin immediately rubbed his throbbing wrists as he brought his arms to his side. Nasher walked back to his gang, who were now all laughing and smiling with each other.

"Let's get out of 'ere, man," Nasher said, bashing his fist against the girl's fist. "Man's bare hungry, and now we got some Ps to get a fat munch."

Nasher and his crew walked past Gavin. Refusing to look at their face as they walked past, Gavin bowed his head, so he was looking at the stony ground. No matter how hard it was, Gavin stopped any tears from emerging until they were gone. Their voices began to get fainter as they walked towards the door to enter the school building.

"Oi Brixton boy!" Nasher shouted.

Gavin slowly turned his head around with a burning rage coursing through his veins like molten lava. Nasher was holding Gavin's iPhone in his hands.

"Here's your phone back." Then, Nasher threw it onto the floor and stamped on it with his right foot. He gave Gavin a devilish grin, flashing his grills.

"Welcome to Hackney. Dickhead."

With those final words, Nasher opened the door to the school building and followed his crew inside.

Gavin could still hear Nasher's faint laughter as his eyes began to sting with tears.

Chapter Six

A boy's first kiss

January 2008

Throughout the rest of the school day, Gavin avoided speaking to anyone.

Feeling like the whole world was now against him, Gavin sat at the back of his Geography class. He was teeming with suppressed rage. The geography teacher, Mr Anderson, was rambling on about something called the world's axis. Gavin was not taking any of it in. His mind was preoccupied with his encounter with Nasher, repeatedly playing the events in his head. What Nasher had done to Gavin had rattled his confidence, but what really hurt Gavin was Yemi's actions. All Gavin kept thinking about was how Yemi had led him to a trap and then abandoned him. Yemi was supposed to be his friend and had betrayed him.

At 5pm, the loud school bell rang across the school corridors. Gavin put on his jacket, picked up his bag and dashed out of the classroom as quickly as possible. All he wanted to do was get home and avoid everyone.

When Gavin walked out the school gates, hundreds of noisy students had engulfed the street. Gavin thought he would not be noticed among the throng of people, but it did not work out that way. As soon as he was on the pedestrian pavement, he heard Yemi's voice.

"Yo, Gavin, hold up," Yemi said. He was hurrying towards Gavin. Kwesi, Andrew, Toby and Carlos were right behind him. Gavin's first thought to seeing the boys coming toward him was to bolt it, but then he decided not to. Now he wanted to confront Yemi about what had happened.

"Bruv, everything good?" Yemi said as soon he and the other boys stopped in front of Gavin.

"Nasher didn't do anything to you?" Kwesi asked, putting his hand on Gavin's shoulder. "That guy is the biggest prick. He only gets away with moving like a big man because everyone is shook of his older brothers."

But Gavin did not care for what Kwesi had to say. He aggressively shoved Kwesi's hands from his shoulder and ignored the shocked expression on Kwesi's face. With his inner rage sizzling, Gavin pushed Yemi hard against his chest. Yemi would have fallen down if not for Kwesi and Toby holding onto him as he stumbled back.

"You boy'd me off, man. You set me up," Gavin said through clenched teeth. "I thought you was my boy, but then you let a next man jack me."

"What?" Yemi said. He looked visibly shocked and hurt. "Nah, it's not like that, fam. I didn't know what Nasher was gonna do to you. His boys just told me he wanted to chat to you and that I should bring him to you. I didn't know he was gonna jack you, I swear."

Gavin shook his head. "Whatever, man, I don't believe you, innit. You handed me over to them and then left me there by myself. You just walked away like some pussyhole."

Yemi opened his mouth to say something, but no words came out. He bowed his head as if he was ashamed of his actions. This only made Gavin more aggravated.

"All of you man should stay away from me, innit," Gavin said in a threatening tone. He slowly stepped backwards as he readied to turn and walk away from the group. "You're not my boys, and I don't need you lot. I don't need anyone."

Not waiting to hear anything more from Yemi or the rest of the boys, Gavin turned away from them and headed to the bus stop. He would get the bus back to the estate alone. Now Gavin finally realised the truth. The only person he could trust at this school was himself.

******

Gavin slammed the door of uncle Reece's flat.

Uncle Reece popped his head out of the kitchen door frame. When he saw Gavin stomping into the flat, he stepped out of the kitchen fully with his hands on his hips.

"Can you not slam my door like that," uncle Reece said, shaking his head at Gavin, who now stood at the foot of the staircase. "And why didn't you respond to my texts or pick up your phone? I am working late at the barbershop tonight and don't have time to cook, so you'll have to order takeaway or eat the leftover food in the fridge."

Hands clenched on the staircase frame, Gavin looked at his uncle, gave him a dismissive look and started walking up the stairs.

"Oi, I am talking to you, nephew. So you respond, understand?"

Gavin stopped on the third step and took a deep breath. The rage ripping through him like a tornado since lunchtime had only increased in its destructive nature, so he had no patience for anyone, including his uncle. "My phone ain't working," Gavin said through gritted teeth. "So I can't order a takeaway or answer calls."

Uncle Reece raised his eyebrows at Gavin. "What do you mean your phone isn't working?"

Gavin took his iPhone, with its smashed screen, and threw it over the staircase banister. It landed with a soft thud on the carpet, a couple of feet away from where uncle Reece stood. "Look for yourself, innit."

Uncle Reece looked at the iPhone on the floor and then back at Gavin. There was a furious look on his uncle's face. "Did you just throw your phone down at me? Have you lost your bloody mind? Whatever this attitude is, you better cut it out right now, nephew. Don't you ever throw something at me again."

Even though it was not Nasher talking, at that moment, uncle Reece's stern voice took on the same tone and sound as Nasher's. That was all it took for the tornado of rage to finally destroy Gavin's hold on his frustrations.

"I hate it here!" Gavin shouted, stamping his feet on the ground. "I hate my school, and I hate living here." Tears had emerged at the edges of Gavin's eyes without his permission.

Uncle Reece now looked taken aback. His earlier face of annoyance had disappeared, replaced by one of concern. "What's going on, nephew? Did something happen at school?"

"I don't belong here!" Gavin shouted again, now feeling the tears pour down his face. "I wish I was back in Brixton with my old friends!" Gavin could feel himself slipping into a full-on sob as he began to hiccup. He lowered his voice. "I miss Jamal. I miss my best friend."

"Gavin…" Uncle Reece stepped forward towards the banister. "I know it's a hard time for you right now. Trust me, I get it, nephew."

Gavin shook his head in anger. "How could you know what it feels like knowing your best friend is never coming back because he's dead *forever*. Jamal is never coming back!"

Uncle Reece closed his eyes and took a deep breath. "I know exactly what that feels like, nephew."

"How do you know!?"

"I also lost someone close to me once, Gavin. And I know what it feels like to be in a new environment. Come sit with me, and we can talk about it." Uncle Reece gestured to the sofa.

Gavin looked at the sofa, then back at his uncle's face. Some part of Gavin wanted to speak to his uncle and finally unload all his supressed rage and sadness that had been building like a Jenga tower since Jamal's murder. But the bitterness Gavin now felt had taken control of him completely. All he wanted to do was hurt someone, so they could feel pain like him.

"Stop acting like you're my dad, " Gavin said, adding extra venom to every word to hurt his uncle. "You're not him, so I don't need to share anything with you."

Instead of becoming angry, which Gavin hoped would happen as he wanted a reaction, uncle Reece nodded his head silently. Still, Gavin could see that he had pinched a nerve. He was satisfied with that and relished in his pettiness.

"Yes, you're right; I am not your dad." Without looking at Gavin, uncle Reece picked up Gavin's broken iPhone without saying a word. He then made his way to the coat rack, grabbed his brown leather jacket, and went to the front door. Before he opened it, he looked back at Gavin with an expressionless face. "There's some leftover curry and rice in the fridge and some chicken wings. I'll get your phone fixed." Saying nothing else, uncle Reece stepped outside and closed the door.

Gavin turned away from the stairs' landing and marched upstairs. As soon as he got into his room, he flung his school bag onto the floor and removed his jacket. He slumped onto his bed, dipped his right hand inside the breast pocket in his blazer, and took out the Charizard Pokémon card. Gavin stared at it for a moment and then began to sob again, floods of tears running down his cheeks and soaking his white, school shirt. He curled up in bed in the foetal position and cried till he fell asleep, clutching the Pokémon card his dead best friend had given him.

******

The following morning, Gavin sat silently with uncle Reece in the car. Neither of them spoke. Gavin glanced at his uncle a few times, but his face was blank as he drove the car and faced the road ahead. *Should he say something? But what could he say?* Gavin decided to remain silent, letting his stubbornness win over. The anger he had felt from yesterday had not completely subsided.

Uncle Reece brought the car to a stop on a road a few yards away from the school. Students were already pouring into the school through the gates with their Nike backpacks or JD string bags over their shoulders. The young minds were beginning another day of learning in class and surviving in the playground.

"Here's your phone. It's fixed," uncle Reece said flatly. He held out a phone to Gavin, who took it from him.

"Thanks," Gavin said, rubbing his hand over the iPhone's smooth screen, which was no longer cracked.

After placing the iPhone in his pocket, Gavin pressed the handle on the door and pushed it open. He looked back at uncle Reece. Paying him no attention, his uncle looked straight ahead at the windshield. Usually, uncle Reece would always wish Gavin good luck every morning before Gavin exited the car to go to school. Gavin could tell that was not going to happen today. Feeling more hurt by his uncle's silent treatment than he thought he would, Gavin stepped out of the car and closed the door.

Clasping the straps on his backpack, Gavin walked towards the school gates. He heard uncle Reece's car speed off behind him.

******

At school, Gavin kept entirely to himself. In his Maths lesson that morning, where he would usually sit next to Yemi, Gavin instead walked right past him and sat at the back of the classroom. Yemi turned around from where he was sitting at the front of the class and looked at him but clearly reading the unfriendly stare Gavin sent him, Yemi turned his head back to the front of the class. He did not look back at Gavin for the rest of the class.

The rest of the day, until lunchtime, Gavin moved through the school like a ghost. He did his best to listen to the teachers. When he was no longer engaged during a lesson, he scribbled drawings of Ferraris and Lamborghinis on his textbooks.

When lunchtime came, Gavin hurried to collect his tray to be served lunch by the always irritable dinner ladies. As he joined the queue of students waiting to get another plate of an unappealing school meal, he noticed Yemi, Kwesi, Andrew, Toby and Carlos ahead of the line. They were talking animatedly to each other. Although he was slightly tempted to join them, he could not pretend he did not miss their lunchtime banter about football, music and girls; Gavin chose to hang back.

So long as Yemi was with them, Gavin would not speak to any of the boys.

After gobbling up his insulting lunch of two slices of hard and crusty pepperoni pizza, Gavin quickly hurried out of the cafeteria. He had decided to spend the rest of his lunchtime in the library, not reading books; that would be insane, but listening to some music on his iTunes. Dizzee Rascal had released his new album, *'Maths + English'*, and Gavin still needed to hear it.

Gavin walked down the long empty corridor which led to the school library on the second floor. He heard footsteps moving quickly behind him and then a female's voice called his name.

"Hey Gavin, please, can you wait."

It was Jamella. Gavin stopped and turned his whole body around to see Jamella walking briskly towards him. Today, she had not worn a skirt but some tight-fitting black trousers and a black school jumper instead of a blazer. Her pink bandanna was wrapped around her curly, dark hair, which reached her shoulders. For some stupid reason, Gavin even found her hair incredibly attractive. Everything about her was flawless, really.

"Are you ok?" she said, stopping right before Gavin. She slightly tilted her head and narrowed her curved lips. Now she looked upset. "I saw you leaving the cafeteria, so I followed you. I have been texting you all day, but you haven't replied to me like you always do. I spoke to Yemi and he said you two aren't speaking to each other and you're blanking him. What's happening?"

Gavin looked away and peered over her shoulder while tapping his feet. A part of him, annoyingly enough as it was, was scared that Nasher and his gang would walk down the corridor and spot him speaking to Jamella.

"Please speak to me," Jamella said, her Barbadian accent melting in Gavin's ears.

Gavin let out a sigh and kissed his teeth in annoyance. "Nasher, your *boyfriend,* said I should stop talking to you, innit. He threatened me and smashed my phone."

Jamella shook her head in disbelief. "He's such a dickhead, that boy. But *Boyfriend?* I am not going out with him."

"Well, that's not what he thinks."

Jamella let out an exasperated sigh. "He asked me out a few weeks ago, and I told him I don't like him in that way and I just wanna be friends. So I don't know why he's telling everyone I am his girl because I am really not."

"I don't want any beef with him, man. Everyone keeps talking about his older brothers, and I ain't trying to get into any arms with some Hackney roadman."

Jamella's features morphed into a frown which oddly made her more cute to Gavin. "So, you're just gonna stop speaking to me because of him. Even when you know that I like you." Jamella quickly put her hand over her mouth as if she had said something she was not supposed to.

But Gavin had heard what she had said as clearly as he saw the sky on a summer afternoon. "You...you like me?" he said, his heartbeat rising as he stared at Jamella's brown eyes. "Like, like me, like me?"

Jamella removed her hand from her mouth and nodded her head sheepishly. She giggled. "Yeah, I like you, like you. Do you…like me, like me?"

At that moment, Gavin thought that Nasher and the rest of his goons could go and suck their mums. Jamella had just said she liked him, and there was nothing on this Earth, not even Hackney gangsters, that would keep him from her. As Jamella stared at Gavin, he knew now was the moment.

Without thinking about it, Gavin stepped closer to Jamella, so they were pressed against each other. Her eyes were half closed and she looked dazed as if she was in a dream and was completely relaxed. Gavin tilted slightly to the side, remembering what he had watched in some romance movie, and leaned in towards her. When his lips met hers, it sent a wave of euphoria across his body. Jamella's lips were as soft, wet and satisfying as he always dreamt they would be. Closing his eyes as he concentrated on the texture of her lips and savoured their taste,

Gavin could not have planned his first kiss any better.

After a minute, but it felt much longer than that, Gavin and Jamella finally detached their lips from one another. Gavin felt dazed as if he had just woken up from a satisfying dream. He had never smoked weed before, only smelt it around the estate and caught a whiff of it everywhere he went in Brixton, but this must be what it felt like when you smoked it. That kiss had gone straight to his head.

"Hey, I've got history class in five minutes, and I've been late every week, so I can't be late today, or I'll get detention," Jamella said. She was holding both of Gavin's hands. "Meet me at Hackney Marshes later; I'll text you. Nasher won't be there. He always hangs out at the McDonald's on the high street anyway."

"Yeah…ok," Gavin mumbled, still feeling disorientated from his first ever kiss from a girl.

"Oh and Gavin."

"Yeah."

"Why are you blanking Yemi?"

The mention of Yemi's name kicked Gavin out of his mental haze, bringing Jamella into sharp focus. He hadn't expected her to ask that question. "Because he boy'd me off, innit."

"What'd you mean?"

"He took me to Nasher at the back of the school and then ducked, leaving me with Nasher and his goons who roughed me up and jacked me. He wasn't even there to back me."

Jamella nodded her head and squeezed Gavin's hands gently. "I get it. But Yemi's a good guy, and he was probably just scared as well and didn't know what that idiot was gonna do. He's one of the few good boys in this school. You want him as a friend. Trust me."

Gavin nodded, although he had been paying more attention to Jamella's lips, which he desperately wanted to kiss again. Jamella let go of Gavin's hand, blew him a kiss and hurried off in the opposite direction.

As he watched her scurry away, her curly hair swaying, Gavin could hardly believe his luck. He had been at Kingsland Academy for less than a month and already he had a girlfriend. Although he had also made enemies with Nasher and his gang, who he would have to deal with, at least he got the girl he wanted.

Hopefully, he would be able to keep hold of her.

Chapter Seven
Battle at the cafeteria

February 2008

Now that Gavin was going out with Jamella, they had decided to keep their relationship a secret between them. Jamella had not even told Mabel. This way, they would not draw Nasher or anyone else's attention at school. At first, Gavin was nervous, not only because he was weary of Nasher catching on that he was dating Jamella, but Gavin had never had a girlfriend before. He had no idea what to expect or what he was supposed to do and had no older brother to show him the ways.

Luckily, things just seemed to continue as they were before with Jamella, only now he got to kiss those gorgeous lips she had. Over the next few days, they would covertly text each other when they were in class. During lunchtime, to avoid arousing suspicion, they did not sit together if they were in the cafeteria at the same time but would still text each other. Their texting mainly consisted of sending each other kisses and saying how much they missed each other. It was the same when they messaged each other on Facebook in the evenings.

The best part about dating Jamella was definitely after school when they would have their secret rendezvous at Hackney Marshes. Away from the boys who would play football in the wide open grass field, Gavin and Jamella had found a secluded enclosure among the leaves and trees. Gavin would sit with Jamella on the grass and listen to her talk. And she loved to talk. About everything. Jamella spoke about her fear of not fitting in because of her strong accent, her complicated relationship with her mum, and the girls she liked and disliked at school. Admittedly, Gavin did not always listen when she talked, not that she noticed. Sometimes he would just nod as she chatted away, patiently anticipating the next chance he would get to kiss her.

But yesterday, during their meetup at Hackney Marshes, Jamella had said something to Gavin that had made him rethink his whole idea of what it was like to be a girl.

Sitting on the wooden lodge beside Gavin, Jamella has been strangely quiet. By now, she would be talking about her social life without barely catching a breath, so Gavin knew something was bothering her.

"Hey baby, are you ok?" Gavin asked, squeezing her hand gently as Jamella cast her eyes down at the trodden leaves. There was a tired look on her face, as if all she wanted to do was curl up in bed and sleep.

Jamella let out a deep sigh. "I am sick of boys." She quickly looked up at Gavin and gave him a warm smile. "Not you, of course. You're different. It's just other guys. They never leave me alone."

"What happened? Is some boy being a prick to you?" Gavin narrowed his eyes and deepened his voice to sound more manly, feeling a strong need to protect his girl.

"No, there's no boy." Jamella took a deep breath. Today I was walking to school with Mabel, and these older guys in a car pulled up next to me; they wined down the car window and said I looked buff in a skirt and that I looked *choong* for my age."

"Oh," Gavin said, not entirely sure how to respond. In his head, he had thought girls liked getting attention from boys. Well, that is what it looked like to him as the girls at school were always giggling as they allowed boys to chase them around the playground and smack their bums with their ties.

As if she had read Gavin's thoughts, Jamella continued. "Some girls like all the attention they get from older men but not me. I feel so uncomfortable when I get attention from them because of how I look. Sometimes, I wish I was like other girls in year 7 who don't have breasts or thighs. At least they don't have all these creepy men randomly making comments about them on the street."

******

Still thinking about what Jamella had said yesterday, Gavin waited in the cafeteria at lunchtime, tray in his hand and ready to collect another unsatisfying free school meal. Then he flinched when he felt someone grab his neck from behind him.

"Man like Brixton boy," came Nasher's threatening voice from behind.

Even with Nasher's right hand gripping his neck, Gavin managed to turn his head just enough to see Nasher's face. He was wearing his signature black and grey cap. Standing behind Nasher was his usual gang. All of them were grinning, clearly enjoying Gavin being tormented.

"I am just getting my lunch, man. Allow me."

"Shut up, blud! Did I say you could speak, though?" Like some pathetic groupies, Nasher chuckled, and his gang did the same thing. Nasher kissed his teeth. "You year 7s are getting too brave at school. Respect your elders; you get me."

When Gavin remained silent, he had hoped Nasher would remove his hand from his neck and go away, but it seemed the dickhead still had more to say.

Nasher leaned into Gavin. With his mouth so close to Gavin's face, he caught a whiff of the smell of cigarettes which irritated Gavin's nostrils. "I hope you ain't been chatting to Jamella," he said, squeezing tighter on Gavin's neck. "I am gonna be speaking to her later today, innit. Man better not see any texts from you on her phone, or you'll see what happens to your face."

Gavin did his best to conceal his nervousness. He made a mental note to remind Jamella to delete all his text messages. Deciding not to speak, in case his voice gave him away, Gavin nodded his head. Nasher removed his hand from Gavin's neck and walked away, barging Gavin's shoulder as he did so.

The girl in Nasher's crew, who Gavin had learned was called Nina, winked at Gavin and slapped him on the shoulder as she stood next to him.

"Thanks for buying us KFC last time. We proper enjoyed that munch." With that, Nina walked off to join the rest of Nasher's group, rolling her head in laughter. Gavin had to take several deep breaths to cool his rage.

After collecting his lunch, today was a chicken pie with watery gravy, lumpy baked beans and some pathetic yoghurt; Gavin made his way to the dinner table. He sat at a table opposite where Yemi, Kwesi and the other boys were sitting. It had been a whole week that Gavin had not spoken to Yemi and the guys. With each passing school day, he missed their company more and more. Jamella had said he should give Yemi another chance. Gavin looked up from his plate and saw Yemi looking at him. He nodded his head at Gavin, and Gavin decided to acknowledge him with a nod back. At that moment, Gavin decided to forgive Yemi for his actions. Sitting by himself at lunch was getting boring anyway.

Just as Gavin stood from the dinner table, getting ready to make his way to Yemi and the other boys, he stopped. Nasher and his goons were now standing directly by Yemi's table. Rather than continue towards them, Gavin hung back and watched Nasher, who had started speaking to Kwesi. Since he was not far away, Gavin could hear their whole exchange.

"Oi, Big Mac, your packed lunch looks decent, still," Nasher said. He was leaning over the table to examine the contents of Kwesi's packed lunch in a transparent, blue plastic container. "Let me take that doughnut, innit. You're too fat anyway, and it's probably gonna give you a heart attack." Nasher grabbed the sugar-coated ringed doughnut from Kwesi's packed lunch as his gang chortled from behind him.

Gavin watched as Kwesi looked down at the table. Kwesi's bottom lip was trembling and he looked like he would cry at any moment. Andrew, Toby and Carlos pretended that the bullying was not occurring, instead choosing to awkwardly continue eating their lunch. But Yemi, sitting next to Kwesi, glared at Nasher.

"Why're you crying, man? I am doing you a favour, Big Mac, saving your life and that," Nasher said. He stuffed the doughnut in his mouth and rubbed his belly. "I can't lie, this doughnut is peng," he said, through mouthfuls.

To Gavin's surprise, Yemi launched from his seat and squared up to Nasher, hands curled into a fist. "You're in year 9, and you're stealing food from year 7s. Do you know how sad that is? I bet you wouldn't act like such a bad man in front of the boys in year 10 or year 11."

Harris, the big black boy wearing a puffer jacket, who Gavin recognised from the day Nasher robbed him, stepped towards Yemi, but Nasher stretched out his hand and shook his head. Harris fell back but he continued to send Yemi a dirty look.

Nasher examined Yemi, who was still squaring up to him. He chuckled. "Yeah, I thought I recognised you when you brought Brixton boy to me. You live on Pembury estate where my auntie lives. I know about your dad, you know." Yemi widened his eyes in surprise and Nasher began to snicker.

"Your dad is a taxi driver. Sometimes he picks up my auntie when she goes shopping. This is why you come to school dressed like a tramp." As he pointed at Yemi's trainers, Nasher began to laugh, and so did the rest of his cohorts. "Look at your creps, man. They look like your dad's slippers. Obviously, your taxi driver dad couldn't afford Adidas, so he had to get you some two-striped fake ones from Primark. If my dad was that poor, I would run away from home."

Yemi grinned at Nasher. "At least I have a dad, innit."

All the laughter coming from Nasher and his goons immediately stopped. Nasher grabbed Yemi by his shirt and pulled him towards him. Possessed by some instinct to protect his friend, Gavin picked up the yoghurt from his tray. There was no thinking; Gavin was acting on pure anger now.

"I dare you to say that again," Nasher said, pressing his forehead against Yemi's. "I'll mash up your face, blud. Remember who you're speaking to, innit."

Gavin lobbed the yoghurt towards Nasher's direction. It soared through the air in one smooth arch before descending and landing, with a splat, on Nasher's black and grey New Era cap. Jamal would have congratulated Gavin on the accuracy of his shot.

A thick, pinkish custard now stained most of Nasher's hat. Some of it dripped onto his school blazer and his black Nike Airforce 1 trainers.

Everything went still as Gavin felt his heart pounding against his chest. Nasher let go of Yemi and pushed him away. With a look of disbelief, Nasher turned his head towards the direction where the projectile yoghurt had come from. His murderous eyes settled on Gavin like a lion ready to rip apart its prey.

"Did you throw that?" Nasher said in a low but ominous voice. He slowly advanced toward Gavin, his eyes burning with anger. "I am talking to you, Brixton boy. Was that you?"

Although a large part of Gavin wanted to run away as Nasher came closer to him, he knew there was no going back.

"Yeah, it was me," Gavin said in a wobbly voice that he hoped sounded defiant to everyone else. "And what?"

Nasher lunged at Gavin, and the two of them were engaged in a tussle. Every pupil in the cafeteria stopped whatever they were doing and turned towards the wrestling match between Gavin and Nasher. Within seconds, the dinner hall transformed into an arena filled with spectators shouting, screaming and cheering as they watched Gavin and Nasher manhandle each other.

"Fight! Fight! Fight!"

Being two years older than Gavin, Nasher naturally had more strength and was using his weight to try and push Gavin to the floor. Using every muscle in his body, Gavin tried to hold on to Nasher and push him away. But it was to no avail. Eventually, Nasher pinned Gavin against one of the dinner tables. As he struggled against Nasher,

Gavin could make out Yemi's desperate voice among the clamour in the cafeteria and Nasher's friends passionately urging Nasher on.

"Let go of him!"

"Bang up that dickhead's face, Nasher!"

Gavin could feel his strength slip away as he was being forced onto the ground by Nasher's arms. As all hoped seemed lost and Gavin feared the worst, Nasher was suddenly flung to the side. In his former place now stood Mrs Churchill, the headmaster. She glared at Gavin with disapproval and shook her head.

"Enough!" Mrs Churchill said, her voice slicing through the air like a sword.

The uproar in the cafeteria died down immediately. Gavin got to his feet, breathing heavily and unruffling his school blazer. Nasher stood behind Mrs Churchill, his face contorted into hatred, and he was fuming as his gang held him back. Mrs Churchill was the only thing separating the two of them.

"I will not tolerate any fighting at Kingsland Academy," Mrs Churchill said, speaking in a loud voice as if she were making a public announcement. She then looked at Gavin and then back at Nasher. "Do I make myself abundantly clear? Any more fighting between you two at this school, and I will expel you both."

Gavin nodded his head and watched as Nasher grudgingly did the same.

"Good. Now both of you will leave the cafeteria separately." Mrs Churchill turned on her heel and left the cafeteria, her air of authority hanging over her as the pupils avoided her gaze.

Yemi, Kwesi, Andrew, Toby and Carlos had all joined Gavin and stood behind him like soldiers ready to defend their captain. Nasher, whose own gang stood behind him, scowled at Gavin with violent intent, resembling an angry rottweiler. Without using his voice, Nasher mouthed, "watch after school. You're a dead man."

With that final warning, Nasher turned away from Gavin and nodded at his gang, beckoning them to follow him. They did as they were instructed and followed Nasher out of the cafeteria. Most students in the hall had returned to eating their school meal, chatting with their friends or playing with their phones as if nothing had happened.

Yemi put his hand on Gavin's shoulders. "You ok, bruv? You held off Nasher, man. I gotta rate you for that."

Kwesi was beaming at Gavin as if he were some guardian angel who had descended from heaven to protect him. "I ain't ever seen anyone stand up to Nasher like that. Thanks, man. I owe you one."

"It's cool," Gavin said, turning to Kwesi and smiling. "Someone had to stand up to that dickhead, man."

"Fam, you're brave," Andrew said, looking at Gavin with a grave expression as if he were talking to someone who had just picked a fight with Mike Tyson in his prime.

"But you just stood up to Nasher. Like, this ain't over, innit.

Chapter Eight
Rumble at the Park
February 2008

Gavin's brief fight with Nasher in the cafeteria had only been an exhibition bout. The real fight would be after school.

Although Gavin had not verbally agreed to fight Nasher again, the unwritten laws of the school playground had already decided that he had to. The news of his impending rematch with Nasher became the main topic of conversation in the classrooms and corridors for the rest of the school day. There was an electrifying excitement among the year 7s and even students in the years above. Although there were always fights happening at Kingsland Academy to settle beefs, nearly every week, the anticipated fight between Gavin and Nasher was different. It was being viewed through the lens of east London verses south London. Brixton against Hackney.

Gavin stood outside the school gates, leaning against the black railings. He was surrounded by dozens of students, primarily boys, including Yemi, Kwesi, Andrew, Toby and Carlos, standing the closest to him. In just over a month, Gavin had become the most talked about pupil at Kingsland Academy. He felt like a celebrity, but not in the way he wanted. Everybody at school was expecting him to fight Nasher. If Gavin refused, nobody at the school would let him forget that he had chickened out especially when he had technically started the beef with Nasher. None of the boys would rate him. He would be labelled a *pussyhole*, a title he did not need hanging over him for the rest of his time at school.

"Fam, whatever happens, we're backing you," Yemi said, putting his hand on Gavin's shoulder. "Man ain't running away this time."

Gavin gave Yemi a weak smile and nodded at him and the rest of the boys, grateful for their support. "Safe, you man. This is long but whatever, let's just do this ting; you get me."

Gavin stepped away from the railings to begin the trek to Hackney Downs Park, where the fight was set to take place, and Nasher was already waiting for him. As Gavin began to move, he saw Jamella run towards him with Mabel close behind her. Jamella flung herself onto Gavin and squeezed him tight, much to the surprise of everyone surrounding them.

"Oh my God, are you ok, baby?" Jamella said, stroking Gavin's braids. "I heard about this fight with Nasher after school at the park . Do you really need to do this?"

"What? Of course he has to," Toby said, looking at Jamella and shaking his head as if she were a naive child. "This is how it has to be, innit."

Mabel, standing beside Jamella, looked at Toby and rolled her eyes. "I don't get you boys," she said, shaking her in disbelief, "why does everything have to end up in a fight with you lot? Can boys not sit down and talk out their disagreements? Is it really that deep?"

"You're saying that like girls don't get into fights," Kwesi said, folding his arms and looking like Gavin's unofficial bouncer. "Girls will rip each other's weaves and eyelashes off over some next boy. It is what it is, innit."

Jamella looked at Gavin and he could see the pleading in her beautiful brown eyes. She took his hands and squeezed them gently. "Baby, you don't have to fight him."

Gavin sighed and shook his head. How he desperately wished that was true. "If I don't fight him, you already know what they will say about me around school. Whatever happens, this beef with Nasher ends today."

******

With a line of at least two dozen Kingsland Academy students behind him, Gavin walked through Hackney Downs Park towards his opponent. It was a slightly chilly afternoon, but the sky was a clear blue, and the sun had decided to show up, too, although it had left its warmth behind. Walking beside Gavin on his right were Yemi, Kwesi, Andrew, Toby and Carlos, and to the left of him were Jamella and Mabel. Although Gavin was feeling the pressure and nerves across his whole body, causing him to sweat a lot in his school shirt, he would have been more scared if he did not have his friends and girlfriend with him.

Nasher stood with his arms folded on a basketball court in the middle of the park. Standing behind him like loyal foot soldiers were at least twenty people. There was his usual crew and some other students from Kingsland Academy. But there were also people not dressed in school uniforms but wore casual clothing. Some of these spectators had their hoods up, concealing their faces. One of the boys on Nasher's side of the court, wearing a camouflage green jacket, had even brought his brown, muscular Pitbull Terrier. The dog was barking ferociously as its handler yanked it back with a pull of its leash.

Taking deep breaths and feeling his heart beat so hard it was like it wanted to shoot out of his rib cage, Gavin stood in the middle of the basketball court. Everyone who had followed him to the park stood at the court's edges. With excited spectators on both ends of the basketball court, Gavin felt like he was about to fight in a WWE cage match. Nasher took off his jacket and school blazer and rolled up the sleeves of his white school t-shirt. Not once did he take his eyes off Gavin, and he had a gleeful smile on his face. This fight was clearly going to fun for him.

Gavin took off his Nike backpack and his school blazer. Yemi ran across the basketball court and took the items from Gavin.

"Bruv, we're here. Remember that, yeah." Gavin looked at Yemi and nodded his head at him.

When Gavin turned his head around to face Nasher, he was already charging towards him. Adrenaline charged through Gavin's body, and he skipped to the side, his shoulder brushing Nasher's outstretched hand curled into a tight fist. Gavin turned around to face Nasher, now standing in the part of the basketball court that Gavin had been standing in. Everyone who surrounded the basketball court had now started cheering and shouting.

The fight had now begun.

"Nasher! Nasher! Nasher!"

"Brixton boy! Brixton boy! Brixton boy!"

Nasher flashed a sinister smile at Gavin. "Where's all that bad boy attitude you had in the cafeteria? Come on, then. Let's see if you year 7s can swing."

Gavin charged at Nasher, throwing his arms wildly at him, screaming his battle cry. Even though Nasher was older than Gavin, he was not much taller.

Nasher had underestimated this fact and had not blocked his face properly, so Gavin's right fist lightly connected with Nasher's left cheek.

"Are you dumb, blud!" Nasher shouted, now parrying Gavin's reckless punches. He grabbed Gavin's right arm to stop him from throwing it around. With his left hand, Nasher then shot his clenched fist straight into Gavin's midriff.

Stumbling back, Gavin howled in agony and held his stomach. He was wincing in pain. Seizing the moment, Nasher grabbed Gavin by the shirt and threw him onto the rough concrete. Gavin landed on his side and rolled on the floor, coming to a stop on his back. The screams from the spectators and the barking from the Pitbull were deafening, and Gavin felt dizzy. Before he even got to his feet, Nasher was already upon again him like a leopard. Now on top of Gavin, Nasher began throwing punches at Gavin and shouting in a rage. Gavin put his hands over his forehead to block Nasher's onslaught of wild jabs. Using as much strength as he could summon, Gavin lifted his right leg and booted Nasher square in his chest. A scream flew from Nasher's mouth as he fell back.

Now free from Nasher, Gavin started to get onto his feet. But before Gavin could fully stand up, Nasher, quickly recovering from Gavin's boot to his chest, charged into him. Wrapping his arms around

Gavin's torso, Nasher threw Gavin off balance and slammed him onto the ground again.

Gavin hit his head hard on the stony concrete. Everything became disorientating, as if Gavin was inside a snow globe that was being shaken rapidly. His vision had become blurry, and then he felt Nasher slap him across his cheek and then slap him again. Each strike from Nasher was raw, relentless and rageful, sending waves of pain across Gavin's face.

"Who's a bad boy now, dickhead," Gavin heard Nasher shout from the top of his lungs as he continued to hit Gavin's face. "I am gonna slap you up like your dad should have done."

Gavin's whole face was throbbing and sore, and his vision was still blurry. In this state, he could not fight back against Nasher's attack. Feeling tears, Gavin closed his eyes and began to cry out.

"Stop, stop, stop!"

The slaps ceased.

With his eyes still closed and his face feeling like it had been dipped in scorching hot water, Gavin heard another male's deep voice in front of him. It was not Nasher speaking but it sounded like an older teenager.

"Oi Nasher, that's enough, man. He's just a kid. Allow this fight, innit. He's already crying, cuz. You won."

As soon as Nasher got to his feet, Gavin felt immense relief. Nasher had used all his weight to pin Gavin to the ground. Someone then grabbed Gavin from underneath his arms and hoisted him up. Although his legs still felt unsteady, his face was burning, and he tasted blood in his mouth, Gavin managed to stand. Finally, he opened his eyes, and his vision returned to normal. Both Yemi and Kwesi were holding him up by his arms.

Nasher stood in front of Gavin. The right sleeve of his now crumpled white school shirt was slightly ripped, but apart from that, he looked unharmed from the fight. He was holding a card in his right hand and waving it around. Gavin was horrified when he realised what Nasher was holding. It was Jamal's Pokémon card.

"Look what fell out of this little dickhead's pocket," Nasher said, raising the Pokémon card in the air to show everyone standing around the basketball court. "He plays with Pokémon cards; allow it. What a neek." Everyone standing by Nasher's side of the court laughed.

"Allow it, please," Gavin said weakly, clutching his stomach with his right arm, with only Yemi supporting him now. "That's mine.

"Don't cry, you little baby," Nasher said with a wide grin that revealed the glistening grills at the bottom of his teeth. "I ain't gonna steal your little Pokémon card because I ain't wasteman, you get me. But I will do this."

"No!"

Nasher tore the Pokémon card in half and then dropped the pieces to the ground. With shaky hands, Gavin picked up the torn Pokémon card. A flood of tears burst from his eyes as Gavin collapsed onto his knees. Jamella, Mabel, Andrew, Toby and Carlos ran towards Gavin who was weeping.

Jamella knelt down beside him and put her arms around Gavin.

"It's ok, baby. It's alright," Jamella said softly into Gavin's ear.

"Oh, is that how it is then?" Nasher said, watching Jamella console Gavin by resting her head on his shoulders. "You're going out with him now, yeah?"

Jamella shot Nasher a fierce glare like he was the most revolting person she had ever seen. "I was never your girl. Can you get that into your thick head?"

Gavin looked at Nasher, and it seemed like he was about to strike Jamella across the face. Instead, Nasher nodded, and his lips curved into a malice smile. "You're gonna regret choosing this wasteman over me, innit. I ain't gonna forget this disrespect, you know that, right?."

Jamella pushed up her upper lip. "Do I look like I care?"

Nina walked up towards Nasher and put her left hand on his shoulder. "Fam, the fight is over. Let's bounce. We need to be at the studio in about half an hour."

"Calm, man's leaving now."

Nasher looked down at Gavin, who was whimpering as he held the ripped Pokémon card. He shook his head in pity as if Gavin was a weak animal he had just put down. "Let this be a lesson to you, Brixton boy. If you ever try it with me again, I promise you the next time, I ain't just gonna slap you up. I am gonna do a lot worse."

Leaving Gavin with that grave warning, Nasher walked off in the opposite direction to join his twenty-strong gang of hoodlums. Making a lot of noise with their laughter and the Pitbull Terrier still barking, Nasher's entourage strutted off the basketball court.

Gavin did not move immediately but remained on the ground, still on his knees. He stared at the torn Pokémon card in the palm of his hand. It was only ripped in half so Gavin could still tape it together. But if Nasher had taken the Pokémon card instead,

Gavin was not sure what he would have done, and he was thankful it had not come to that.

Chapter Nine

The cruelty of a rejected boy

February 2008

Nasher leaned against the swivel chair in the recording studio.

Using the fingers in his right hand, Nasher crushed small, hard chunks of weed in the palm of his left hand. In front of him, in a small separate room called the isolation booth, Harris recorded a grime track. Nasher could see Harris through a transparent soundproof window. Large, black headphones, almost half the size of the average person's head, were placed over Harris' ears. In front of Harris was a mic attached to a long stool. He was spitting rapid-fire bars over a melancholic and sparse grime beat with all the energy and bravado of a seasoned MC like Skepta or JME. Out of everyone in his gang, Harris was probably the best MC, secondly only to Nasher, of course.

Nasher poured the contents in his palm into the rizla paper and licked the sticky part of the paper so it would hold together. Finally, he rolled the thin, tightly compacted rizla in his fingers into a cylinder-shaped joint. After he had rolled up the joint, Nasher inspected his handiwork. Rolling a good joint took true craftsmanship, the same way being a good MC took true craftsmanship. It required skill and artistry. Nasher's two older brothers had shown him how to roll a joint when he was around ten years old, and he had been smoking weed ever since.

Nasher turned on his swivel chair to face Nina, who was sitting on another swivel chair beside him. All of his gang were in the recording studio in Dalston. They were chilling in the control room, where the sound engineer mixed and mastered the tracks. The air in the room was heavy with the satisfying smell of weed and McDonald's. Skilla and K Dot were sitting on a brown sofa, both with McDonald's brown paper bags between their legs. They were wolfing down their fries and slurping on milkshakes. The sound engineer, a sixteen-year-old British Chinese boy from Bethnal Green, named Timothy Wong, but everyone called him 'Wong', sat by the control panel in front of the isolation booth. The control panel contained dozens of buttons and a large monitor screen in front of him. Using music software, Wong could see the skeleton and meat of a song visualised by block squares. Wong had at least twenty chicken nuggets in front of him in five separate boxes. Everyone in the recording studio was high and eating fast food. For Nasher, this was the perfect environment for creating banging grime riddims.

"Oi Nina, I beg you pass me your lighter," Nasher said.

"Yeah, of course. Say nuffin, my G." Nina dipped into the inner breast pocket in her school blazer and withdrew a transparent blue lighter.

Nasher took the lighter from Nina and sparked the joint by lighting its tip with the small flame from the lighter. He gave the lighter back to Nina, placed the joint in his mouth and took the first toke.

"I still can't believe Brixton boy started crying today," Nina said, chuckling. She took the joint from Nasher, who held it towards her for her to take. Nina took one toke of the joint, closing her eyes briefly in satisfaction, before continuing. "He had to get banged. These youngers can't be allowed to move too brazen at school. Today was a warning to the years below us not to try it and know their place, you get me."

"I personally think you went too easy on him, Nasher," K Dot mumbled through mouthfuls of his Big Mac, crumbs falling onto his school trousers. "You should have proper mashed up my man's face. He would have gone to school the next day looking like Freddy Krueger's son."

Nasher chuckled as he took the joint from Nina that she had passed back to him. "It's minor. After today, Brixton boy would be an idiot to try and step to man again. I'll slice him up if he tries it with me again." Nasher took a long toke from the joint, inhaled and then blew thin puffs of smoke into the air. He reclined on the swivel chair, feeling the effects of the weed dull his senses and relax his body, making him feel submerged in a warm bath. Smoking weed was the only way Nasher could relax, especially living in a place as wild as Hackney.

"Wagwan for that Jamella girl though?" Nina said, looking at Nasher. "She's such a hoe, and how is she gonna chat to you so rude in front of bare man. You know that's a violation, cuz."

Nasher nodded his head in agreement. Although he was disappointed that Jamella had chosen Brixton boy over him, how she spoke to him really angered him. If the idea he had to get revenge on her had not entered his head, Nasher would have given her a swift backhand there and then on the basketball court. How dare she have the audacity to speak to him in such a manner. But his plan to get revenge on Jamella was more fun and humiliating than any slap he would have given her.

"Don't worry, she ain't getting away with that." Nasher took another toke from the joint and then passed it to Nina again. "I am gonna teach her a lesson, you get me. Man already knows what I am gonna do to her."

Nina pulled on the joint. "Oh swear? What are you gonna do then?"

Nasher smirked at Nina. He sat up and bent down to reach the floor. He was looking for his notepad, where he always jotted down his verses. Thirty minutes ago, he had written some new lyrics. He picked up the notepad and gave it to Nina. "Turn to the latest page and read my bars, innit."

Holding the joint in her left hand, Nina flipped through the pages of the notepad until she got to the latest page with writing on it. Silently, as if in deep concentration, Nina read the lyrics on the page. Once she had finished, she looked up at Nasher. There was an astonished look on her face as if she couldn't quite believe what she had just read. "These lyrics are mad, fam. Are you gonna actually record this?"

"Of course I am. Like I said, I gotta teach her a lesson, innit."

Nasher took his notepad from Nina and then stood up. He walked over to Wong and put his hand on his shoulder. "Oi Wong, tell Harris to finish up now. I wanna record my song, innit."

After Harris had left the isolation booth, Nasher stepped in to record his song. Feeling the buzz of excitement that he got when he was about to record a song, Nasher bounced on the spot and placed the big headphones over his ears. He put his notepad on a stand and flicked open to the page where he had written his newest lyrics.

"You ready to record the first take, bruv?" came Wong's voice from the headphone.

Nasher gave him a thumbs up from the isolation booth. Wong nodded his head, pressed a few buttons, and twisted a few dials on the control panel.

The grime beat slowly started to play from the headphones. The rhythm sailed through Nasher's ears, and he began to feel the tempo and tone of the riddim, nodding his head aggressively as if the instruments within the song had possessed him. You needed to formulate how you would attack the beat with your lyrics and flow. For Nasher, this part was essential for making a big tune. If you got this part right, then DJs would wheel up your track in clubs and radio stations.

The minute the drop in the riddim happened, and the central part of the beat started, Nasher was sufficiently psyched up. He opened his mouth and started rapping fast, easily spraying his lyrics within the flow of the beat's rhythm and tempo.

It only took a single take for Nasher to get it right. He was not recording a song to be played on the radio, but just a basic diss track. After he had recorded the tune, Nasher removed the headphones and hung them on the mic stool. He put his right hand in the air, formed the shape of a gun with it and made a "brap, brap" sound. Everyone in the control room laughed. He took his notepad and left the isolation room.

"Fam, that track was a mad ting," Wong said, grinning at Nasher as he came to stand next to him.

"I don't know who this girl is, but damn, bruv, you didn't hold back. You were savage."

Nasher nodded his head, smiling. "So what you telling me, Wong? Can you get it mixed and mastered today?"

"Of course, G. Light work, you get me. I'll send you the MP3 file this evening."

That was perfect. Once Nasher had the file from Wong, he would upload it onto Facebook and YouTube tonight and message it to a few people at school on his Blackberry. By tomorrow morning, the song would be circulating around the school.

Jamella Greenwood had no idea what was coming to her. Nasher rubbed his hands in glee, knowing he was about to cause a significant stir at school tomorrow. Jamella had shown him disrespect today, and now she was about to get her comeuppance.

******

School life can be such a funny place.

After all the hype and noise surrounding the fight between Gavin and Nasher, when Gavin returned to school the next day, nobody cared about it anymore. It was almost like it had never happened. People had moved on quickly, and the classroom and playground discussions resumed their usual topics: Who was going out with whom? Which school was Kingsland Academy beefing with? And which gangs from the various estates in Hackney were feuding.

The only noticeable difference for Gavin after yesterday's fight was that many of the boys were no longer giving him a screw face or eyeing him suspiciously. Whenever Gavin was in his lessons or walking in the corridor with Yemi, the other schoolboys nodded respectfully at Gavin when they saw him. Even though he had lost the fight with Nasher, the fact that Gavin had not run away like a coward or told the teachers about it earned him respect from the boys. It also attracted further admiration from the girls. Like every school in the ends, there were only three ways a boy gained respect at school. He either got into a fight and held his own against his opponent or he was very good at sports or dating one of the fittest girls at the school. So far, Gavin was doing reasonably well on all three accounts, so the fight with Nasher had been a necessary evil to cement his reputation among his peers. The unwritten laws of secondary school life for a boy were brutal.

Gavin collected his free school meal in the cafeteria. He made his way to the dinner table where Yemi, Kwesi, Andrew, Toby and Carlos were sitting and eating their lunch.

"How are you feeling, man?" Yemi said, bashing his fist against Gavin's outstretched knuckles as Gavin sat down.

"Safe, I am good, bruv," Gavin said, sitting opposite Yemi. After bashing his fists with Kwesi and the other boys, Gavin began eating the soggy spaghetti Bolognese on his plate.

"You got a lot of ratings yesterday for fighting Nasher," Kwesi said, a string of spaghetti hanging from his mouth. "Your beef with him is squashed now, and I don't think he even cares you're going out with Jamella, you know."

"Yeah, hopefully. But he's still a dickhead, though," Yemi said. "One day, Nasher is gonna try it with the wrong person; just watch, innit. There's always someone bigger than you in the ends. His two brothers aren't the only bad man on road."

"Yeah, I hear that," Gavin said, nodding his head at Yemi. "But, to be honest, I just wanna move on from it, innit. I don't even wanna speak about him anymore."

Moving on from Nasher, the boys began discussing the last action-packed episode of Dragonball Z. As they debated Goku's and Vegeta's Super Saiyan power levels, Mabel came to the boy's table. But instead of sitting down, Mabel decided to stand. Gavin and the other boys stopped their discussion and looked up at her. She had a deeply concerned look.

Yemi, who now looked very worried because Mabel seemed very worried, was the first to address her. "Hey, Mabel, what's good? Are you alright?"

"Nah, not really, Yemi," Mabel said, shaking her head. She now looked distraught. "Have you guys not heard the song yet?

The boys all gave each other quizzical looks. Gavin shook his head. "Song? Nah, what song?"

Mabel let out a sigh. She reached into her school blazer and pulled out her Blackberry phone. "Listen to this, innit." Mabel put her phone on the table and pressed a button. A song started to play.

The beat of the song was one you would associate with grime, the most popular music genre in every London school right now, thanks to Channel U and SBTV on YouTube. At first, Gavin and the boys nodded their heads to it, feeling the beat but their smiles quickly twisted into frowns as soon as the MC on the track started spitting his bars. Although the voice was faster and sounded even more menacing, it was unmistakeably Nasher's voice. Gavin leaned towards the phone to better hear Nasher's lyrics.

Jamella Greenwood

Mabel pressed a button on her Blackberry, and the song stopped playing. Everyone immediately looked at Gavin. At first, Gavin was deadly silent as his mind processed what Nasher had just said about his girlfriend in his lyrics. Then a rage started to build within him, and his breathing became heavier.

"Yo, Gavin. Bruv, are you ok?" Yemi said with a concerned tone.

Gavin stood up from the dinner table with such force that he almost knocked over Kwesi, sitting next to him. He curled his hands into a fist

"Where's Jamella?" Gavin demanded in a harsh voice, turning to look at Mabel.

Mabel shook her head, and the expression on her face grew more troubled. "I don't know where she is. I have been calling her phone for an hour, but she's not picking up."

Gripped with a potent mix of outright anger and fear, Gavin dashed out of the cafeteria.

"Yo, Gavin, where you going!" Yemi shouted as Gavin left the dining hall, but he ignored him.

Walking through the school's bottom floor corridor in haste, Gavin took out his iPhone and called Jamella. It rang for a minute before going to her voicemail. Still trying to ring her, his phone pressed into his left ear; Gavin walked up the stairs to the school's second floor. Teachers and students walked past him, some giving him a side eye, but everyone might as well have been invisible to Gavin. All he cared about was finding Jamella.

Again her phone went to voicemail. *Where was she? Why wasn't she picking up?* Gavin's heartbeat was on overdrive.

He tried her phone again for the sixth time. As he walked past the yellow door of the girls' toilets, he heard a phone ringing from inside. Gavin took two steps back and looked at the bathroom door. *Was that her phone?* Gavin called Jamella's number again. Sure enough, the phone rang again inside the girls' toilet. No way was it a coincidence. Looking in both directions to ensure no one was looking, Gavin pushed open the door and entered the girl's toilets.

The boys' toilets at Kingsland Academy immediately attacked your nose with the smell of urine. The floors were always littered with crisp wrappers, cigarette buds, and occasionally used condoms. By contrast, the girls' toilets smelt and looked like they were cleaned every hour. Thankfully, there were no girls in the bathroom when Gavin entered. There was a row of four yellow-coloured cubicles. Gavin could make out someone's black Reebok trainers and white socks in the last cubicle. "Jamella?" Gavin shouted, walking into the middle of the toilet.

"Gavin, is that you?" came Jamella's feeble and quiet voice. She sounded like she had been crying, and Gavin heard her sniff.

"Yeah, it's me, babe."

Jamella burst into sobs. Gavin dashed towards the cubicle and opened the door. Jamella was sitting on the floor with her knees and face buried in her folded arms. Although there was little room inside the cubicle, Gavin sat beside his girlfriend and put his arms around her. Jamella raised her head and turned to look at Gavin. Her eyes were bloodshot, and her mascara, which she sometimes wore to school although girls were not allowed to wear make-up, was badly smudged. Even her pink lip gloss was fading. She buried her head into Gavin's chest and started sobbing again.

"I…I…can't believe he said those things about me," Jamella said between sniffs and tears. "Did…you…hear…the…song?"

Gavin nodded his head. "Yeah, I heard it."

"I've never…never…done any of those things to him that he said I did in the song," Jamella said, her voice cracking. "Please, believe me, Gavin. I am not…I am not loose like that. Now everyone…all the girls are laughing at me. They're all saying I have herpes and swallow because I love the taste of cum. Why are people so mean in this school?"

Jamella's whole body shook as her tears soaked Gavin's white school shirt. He stroked her hair and held her tighter. The distress in Jamella's voice only poured more gasoline onto Gavin's burning rage. Every time Nasher's face flashed in his mind, he clenched his hands into a fist till it hurt. His beef with Nasher was not over. Far from it.

"Of course I believe you, baby. And trust me, Nasher ain't gonna get away this," Gavin said, kissing Jamella's forehead. "I swear on my mum's life, he's gonna pay."

Chapter Ten

Payback

February 2008

"Alright then. So I am guessing you lot wanna know why we're here, innit?"

Gavin stood in front of a row of computer monitors in one of the school's computer rooms. Yemi, Kwesi, Andrew, Toby and Carlos stood in a horizontal line facing Gavin. Also in the room were Mabel and Jamella, who stood next to each other. School had already finished. Most pupils had either gone home, retreated to one of the local parks to play football or roamed the streets of Hackney to cause mischief and trouble. But Gavin and the rest of the group in the computer room did not have time today for any of that.

They were going to plot a plan of revenge.

"This is about Nasher, isn't it?" Carlos said, hands in his pockets and his in-ear headphones dangling around the neck of his red Adidas hoodie.

Gavin nodded his head. "Yeah, it's about that dickhead. Nasher has been giving me trouble since I moved to Hackney. But not just me but almost everyone in this room."

The eyes in the room stared back at him intensely, and Gavin felt like some rebel leader giving a rousing speech to his freedom fighters.

"How long are we gonna let him terrorise us? It's time he got his karma, you get me. It's time someone bullied him for once."

"Yeah, that all sounds very nice, bruv, reh teh teh. But how you gonna bully him though?" Toby said, shaking his head. "Nasher is in year 9 and he's crazy. Bro, you got into a fight with him three days ago, and you got merked. Did you forget?"

Gavin snorted and glared at Toby. "Yeah, so what? Does that mean man's gonna be shook of him forever?"

"It's not just Nasher," Andrew interjected, stepping towards Gavin. "It's also his brothers. The Nash twins are ruthless and are seen as the top boys in the London Fields estate. Everyone is shook of them. They can go anywhere in Hackney, to any estate and postcode, and no one would touch them. That's how feared they are in the streets."

"Yeah, I hear all that," Gavin said, walking diagonally in front of the group like a general planning his attack. "But we still have to do something, innit. Listen, yeah, I've got a plan to get back at Nasher, and we don't have to fight him or anything."

"Nah, I ain't backing it, Gavin," Carlos said swiftly, throwing his hands in the air. "Whatever your plan is, good luck, cuz. But I ain't trying to end up getting shanked, you get me."

Carlos nodded his head at Gavin and left the room.

"Yeah, I am with Carlos, man," Toby said. "Going against Nasher is a death wish. He's a

London Fields roadman. It's not worth it, bruv."
Toby turned around and left the room.

"I ain't even gonna lie; Nasher just scares me,"
Andrew said, shrugging his shoulders. "I am a
pussy, and I admit it. So, good luck, Gavin, with
whatever your plan is. But please don't die, innit."
Andrew turned around and left the room.

Now the only people remaining were Yemi,
Kwesi, Mabel and Jamella. The ones who had not
deserted the cause. Not yet, anyway. Gavin raised
his chin and scanned each of their faces. "What you
lot telling me then? You backing me or not?"

Yemi stepped forward. "Man's with you all the
way, bruv."

"Me too, babe," Jamella said, smiling at Gavin as
she stepped forward.

Mabel cocked her head back in shock as she
looked at her friend as if she had suddenly
transformed into a different person. "Really,
Jamella?" she said, "so you're a bad girl now,
yeah?"

Jamella shot her friend a fierce look. "I am not gonna let Nasher get away with what he said about me in that song. No way. So yeah, I am gonna be a bad girl."

Gavin grinned at Jamella's rude girl attitude, especially as she said it in that sweet Barbadian accent of hers.

Mabel rolled her eyes and shrugged her shoulders as she stepped forward. "Fine, whatever. I guess I am in, then."

Only Kwesi now remained standing behind everyone else. As he played with his fingers, his hulking frame looked like a timid giant. "I don't know about this," he said, avoiding Gavin's face and looking at the floor instead. "The other guys aren't wrong about Nasher and his big brothers, you know. My three older brothers have told me stories about the Nash twins. They kidnapped people in the ends. People who mess with them go missing."

Yemi turned around to face Kwesi. "Big K, how many times has Nasher called you fat and jacked your lunch? Doesn't that get to you?"

Kwesi looked at Yemi and scrunched his face. He looked like he was having an internal battle with himself. His facial expression resembled someone struggling to take a dump in the toilet. "Yeah, Nasher's bullying does get to me," Kwesi said, "but still, are you sure this is the right thing to do? Should we really retaliate?"

"Yes, we should, Big K," Gavin said bluntly. "Nasher is gonna get what he deserves for bullying you. For bullying all of us."

"Yeah, fam. So stop standing there looking confused and join us, man," Yemi said.

Knowing he was defeated, Kwesi sighed and stepped forward to stand next to Yemi. "Ok fine, I am in."

Gavin nodded his head and observed his crew. Now that he had them on his side, he could execute the plan he had been constructing in his head for most of the day. It was fool proof and designed to cause maximum embarrassment to Nasher and damage his rep at school.

"Alright, listen. So here's what we're gonna do."

******

Instead of following the other boys to play football at Hackney Downs Park at the end of the school week, Gavin, Yemi and Kwesi got onto the 236 from Shacklewell Lane, heading to Hackney Wick.

While Gavin and Yemi were excited about the plan to get revenge on Nasher, Kwesi kept shaking his head in disapproval throughout the bus journey. But Gavin ignored Kwesi's doubts. With Kwesi's bulky stature, Gavin would have thought he would be less cautious about everything, but it was almost the opposite.

When the bus reached Broadway Market, Gavin, Yemi, and Kwesi alighted the bus. Located on the street sandwiched between Haggerston and London Fields, Broadway Market was just one of the many popular markets across Hackney borough.

With Yemi and Kwesi walking by his side, Gavin strolled through the busy market. The bustling energy and the noise of traders haggling with customers were not too different from what Gavin experienced when he followed his mum to Electric Avenue in Brixton. Walking through Broadway market, Gavin observed the variety of clothes on display, from African-inspired dresses to fake designer brands. They hung from rows of metal hanger racks, with interested shoppers feeling the fabrics and imagining how they would look on them. Dozens of market stalls carved out the marketplace. Its owners were selling everything, from meat produce, freshly baked bread and cakes and the rarest spices, which tickled Gavin's nostrils when he walked past the stalls. At one of the market corners, standing in front of the Cat and Mutton pub, a middle-aged white man with thin white hairs on his scalp like a cat's whiskers was playing the saxophone. People threw coins into a hat next to his feet. Feeling the music, Gavin tossed a pound coin into the cap before moving on with Yemi and Kwesi.

"Yo, Gavin, that's the shop I was talking about," Yemi said, pointing his finger.

Gavin's eyes followed the direction of Yemi's finger to a small shop a few feet away. It was a fancy dress shop, and there were not many people entering the shop or coming out of it. But it would sell the masks needed to pull off Gavin's revenge plot.

"Alright, let's go inside," Gavin said, making his way to the shop and beckoning Yemi and Kwesi to follow him with a wave of his hand.

The shop's interior was filled with every fancy dress costume and accessory you could think of. There were the Disney princess costumes, the Marvel and DC superhero outfits and the expected masks and get-ups for Halloween. Gavin looked in the direction of the shop where the Halloween costumes and accessories were displayed. Something immediately caught his eye. Hanging from a plastic rack were a couple of goblin masks with long noses, pointy ears and fake teeth shaped like daggers. In a twisted way, Gavin felt like the masks were speaking to him, telling him they would serve him as he carried out his revenge against his enemy. Gavin walked towards the masks and took one from the plastic rack. He examined it, rubbing his hand over the shape of the demon mask.

"What you thinking?" Yemi asked as he came to stand beside Gavin, with Kwesi following from behind.

A devilish smile formed on Gavin's face as he held the demon mask in his hands. "I think these masks are perfect, bruv. Nasher is gonna wet his pants."

After purchasing the masks for himself and Yemi, who did not have money for one, and Kwesi bought one with his own money, the three of them headed out of the fancy dress shop. They spent another thirty minutes purchasing the remaining items for the revenge plan. Once their shopping spree was done, Gavin, Yemi and Kwesi took the 254 to Amhurst Road in Hackney Downs. Once they got off the bus, they made their way to Dixy chicken, their bellies growling for food.

"I can't wait to see the look on Nasher's face when he sees us in those masks," Gavin said, dipping a piece of chip into the small, round plastic container filled with creamy burger sauce.

Gavin was sitting on a bench inside the Dixy chicken shop, with Yemi and Kwesi facing him. All three had ordered four wings, chips and a can of coke with burger sauce; it was a perfect and affordable meal for any east Londoner for only one pound and fifty pence.

"It's gonna be jokes," Yemi said, biting off a piece of his chicken wing. "We're gonna record the whole thing and upload it on Facebook." Yemi raised his coke can to Gavin while Kwesi shook his head. "You got a sick mind, bruv. I wouldn't have thought of this, so I salute you."

Gavin kicked his feet up and nodded his head, impressed with himself. He had to admit, it was a perfect revenge plan, and if they pulled it off, and they would, Nasher's reputation would be completely ruined and he would know what it feels like to be humiliated. A potent taste of his own punishment.

"The way you man are just bussing jokes about what we're going to do is actually jarring," Kwesi said, having finished his food already. "I don't think you two are fully deeping this. Nasher is not only from London Fields, but his big brothers run the estate. If Nasher finds out what we did to him and gets his brothers involved…."

"He's not going to find out," Gavin said, cutting off Kwesi with a sharp tone. "We're wearing masks. So as long we don't bait ourselves up by shouting each other's name or something, we're good, Big K. Just make sure you man are ready on Sunday afternoon because Jamella will be at the park."

While Kwesi looked down at his empty chip box, looking like a soldier forced to go to war, Yemi looked like a soldier who could not wait to enter the battlefield. He bashed his fists against Gavin's.

"Don't worry, bruv. We'll be ready, innit," Yemi said.

******

It was a late afternoon on Sunday.

Gavin hurtled down the staircase with his Nike backpack strapped onto his back and wearing black combat trousers, a black hoodie, and his old black Puma trainers. He jumped over the last two steps onto the landing. Today was the day he was going to carry out the wicked revenge plan he had concocted against Nasher. Today was payback time.

"Hey, uncle Reece!" Gavin shouted as he stood by the front door. "So it's ok for me to take the bike out, yeah?"

Topless, so his surprisingly ripped build and slightly hairy chest were on display, uncle Reece emerged from the kitchen. He had been chopping up some oxtail meat for tonight's dinner. Uncle Reece scrutinised Gavin's attire, and he narrowed his eyes. "Where the *rassclaat* are you going dressed like a bank robber, and why is your bag so big?"

"It's just football stuff," Gavin said, bouncing on the spot impatiently. He did not have time for all this chat. "I am gonna be in goal, so I am covering up my whole body." Gavin hoped that was a convincing enough lie not to raise further suspicions.

Uncle Reece inspected Gavin further but relented with a sigh. "You better not be lying to me, nephew."

"Why would I lie?"

"Whatever. Make sure you bring back that bike in one piece, and I want you in the house by 7pm at the latest. You need to have your dinner and get ready for school tomorrow."

After waving goodbye to his uncle, Gavin opened the flat door and closed it shut as he stepped outside. While there was a slight breeze, the sky was a clear blue, and there was still a lot of daylight. It was a perfect day for filming footage on your phone.

In front of Gavin stood an old, black BMX bike leaning against the guard railings in front of the flat. Uncle Reece had found the BMX bike dumped in a garbage heap at the back of his barbershop two days ago. He had brought it back to the flat and repaired it for Gavin.

To ensure the BMX bike was in perfect condition, as it needed to be if this revenge plot was to go smoothly, Gavin hopped onto the bike's saddle. He positioned himself comfortably on the seat and began to peddle along the front porch, passing the other flats at the bottom of the block. The peddles worked fine, the bike chain was intact, and the front breaks were in order. It was perfect for making a clean getaway.

Gavin hopped off the BMX and took it down onto the main enclosure in the estate in front of the parking bays. As he rested the bike against a brick wall, he heard the sound of walking feet and tyres rubbing the ground. He turned to his right and saw Yemi and Kwesi coming towards him. They were dressed in almost identical clothing, and each pushed their own BMX bike as they walked towards him. Both boys stopped in front of Gavin and, holding their bikes with one hand, bashed their fists against Gavin's.

"You ready to do this, yeah?" Gavin said, looking at Yemi and Kwesi. While Yemi looked thrilled, Kwesi wore a worried expression, as if a bunch of ghosts were hovering above his head.

"Man's ready, bruv," Yemi said, nodding his head. "You got all the stuff, yeah? Where're the masks?"

"Oh yeah, the masks." Gavin removed his backpack and knelt down beside his BMX. He unzipped his Nike backpack. Inside were three goblin masks they had bought on Friday. What made the bag so bulky was the canister and the three two-litre cartons of milk inside. Gavin took out the three green-coloured goblin masks, gave one to Yemi and Kwesi, and held the last one in his hand.

As Gavin zipped up the bag and stood up, he heard a pinging sound from his iPhone. Gavin took it out of his pocket and went to his messages. Mabel had sent him a text.

Jamella is at d park nw. Nasher is gna meet her at the bsktball court in 10 mins. Leave nw

"Is that Mabel??" Yemi said.

"Yeah. She said Jamella is already at the park, and Nasher is gonna link her at the basketball court in ten minutes." Gavin looked at Yemi and gave him a grin. "Alright, let's go. We gotta get there before Nasher does or this whole ting flops, you get me."

As Gavin and Yemi climbed onto their bikes, Kwesi hesitated. His eyes darted from Gavin and then to Yemi. He scratched his short afro hair. "It's not too late to allow this, you man. We don't have to do this, you know."

Before Gavin could respond, Yemi kissed his teeth loudly and shook his head. "We ain't got time for this, Big K. Come on, fam, we're doing this. Jamella is already at the park. You're being long right now. Allow it."

"Alright, whatever." Not the first time, Kwesi let out a regrettable sigh and threw his hulking frame onto his BMX. "Come, let's go then."

Gavin pulled the goblin mask over his face and put his hoodie up. Yemi and Kwesi followed suit. With their faces concealed and hoodies over their heads, Gavin, Yemi, and Kwesi looked like a demonic trio from hell. They cycled out of the estate and made their way to Hackney Downs park, ready to carry out their revenge on Nasher.

******

Listening to Ghetts' classic riddim *'Don't phone me'* through his Sony Ericsson in-ear headphones, Nasher bopped through Hackney Downs park. He was dressed in True Religion bootcut jeans and wore a white Ed Hardy hoodie with a big, silver chain swinging around his neck.

Nasher was definitely feeling himself today. It had been a good weekend for him, and it might get better. Last night he had been at one girl's shoobs in

Stock Newington with his gang. At the house party, he had been feeling one girl he recognised as one of the year 11 girls at Kingsland Academy. After moving to her and chatting her up for a bit, she had led him to the bathroom away from everyone, closed the doors and gave him head. It was the first time Nasher had done anything sexual with an older girl.

If that was the only highlight of the weekend, Nasher would have been satisfied. But then, out of the blue, Jamella had sent him a text this morning, saying she wanted to link up. At first, Nasher was sceptical. Why would she want to link up after he released a diss track about her? But then, she started flirting with him and sending him dirty messages. Nasher's two older brothers once told him that some girls liked boys more when mistreated by them. It was twisted, but Nasher had met some freaky girls through his two older brothers. Nasher figured that Jamella was one of these freaks. It was always the quiet ones, after all. It looked like Brixton Boy was not bad enough for her. But Nasher definitely would be.

Nasher saw Jamella standing by the empty basketball court. As he approached her and she gave him a naughty grin, Nasher had to bite his lip. Jamella was looking extra saucy today. Usually, Nasher did not really move to year 7 girls. Yet even the older boys at school knew Jamella was on a different level, so no boy in his year cussed him for chasing after her. When she was older, Nasher could easily see Jamella as a fashion model. Today, she was wearing tight, black jeans which fitted nicely around her developing curves. She wore her pink bandanna and a denim jacket over her purple crop top, revealing her flat stomach.

"I was thinking you was gonna par man off," Nasher said, standing in front of Jamella. He crossed his arms over his chest and put his hands by his crotch. "But you're actually here. Thought you was a doing a ting with Brixton boy, nah?"

Jamella shrugged her shoulders. "I was, but he was getting boring. I was missing you." Jamella stepped closer to Nasher until she was resting against him. She put her arms around his torso.

Nasher, taller than her by around five inches, looked down at her. "Nah, you're weird, you know. Man dropped a diss track about you, and this makes you like me more?"

"Yeah, I don't know why." Jamella shrugged her shoulders. "I like my bad boys."

Nasher knew it. Jamella was a freak. He raised her chin with his right finger so she looked up at him. Her perfectly shaped lips, not too full or too small, were just asking to be kissed. Nasher leaned his head forward and gave Jamella a full kiss with his whole mouth absorbing hers, and she did not resist. Just as Nasher was about to stick his tongue down her throat, he heard someone aggressively call his name.

"Oi Nasher, you prick!"

Having grown up in Hackney all his life, Nasher knew if someone called you out like that, you were in trouble. He pushed Jamella away from him and looked to his right. When he saw what was coming towards him, he almost wet his Calvin Klein boxers. Three boys in hoodies and wearing green demon masks were speeding towards him on BMX bikes. The boy at the front was holding some kind of canister in his hand.

Nasher turned around and sprinted the other way. Heart racing, he ran as fast as his legs could go. Then he was knocked over by one of the bikes, which crashed into him hard from the side. Screaming in agony, Nasher collapsed onto the floor, landed on his side and rolled on his back. The sound of metal hitting the ground reached Nasher's ears and he realised the demon mask boys had dismounted their bikes. Still lying on the grass with his right hand over his throbbing left rib, Nasher opened his eyes to find himself looking up at the sky. Suddenly, one of the demon mask boys, the one holding the canister, appeared in his view. The demon mask boy sprayed something in his eyes from the canister. Before Nasher could even think about rushing to his feet and legging it, his eyes burned with a painful sting.

"Arghhh, my eyes. I can't see!" Nasher screamed, rubbing his eyes in agony as he rolled on the grass. Tears started to stream down his cheeks. "Help me, I can't see."

"Yo, take out your phone and record this. I am about to pour it," Nasher heard one of the demon mask boys say. Being in so much pain from his irritated eyes and terrified for his life, Nasher could not concentrate on the voices of his attackers to know if they sounded familiar.

What happened next almost put Nasher in shock. Gallons of some sort of cold liquid were poured all over his face. When he tasted the liquid, he realised it was milk. Still blind and his eyes stinging badly, Nasher spluttered and gasped for air as the milk kept being poured all over him. So much milk kept pouring over Nasher's face that he could not speak to beg his attackers to stop. Finally, the steady spew of milk drowning his face ended.

His whole face and clothes now soaked with milk, Nasher lay on the grass, rubbing his stinging eyes as he breathed heavily, desperately taking in some air. Shaking with shock, Nasher could hear the demon mask boys get on their bikes. They were laughing as they cycled away. It was that laughter that he would not forget. It etched onto his memory like a tattoo.

He heard Jamella's panicking voice. "Oh my god, are you ok?" She knelt beside him now and helped him get to his feet. "Who were those boys?"

As Nasher stood up, he tried to open his eyes, but the pain was excruciating, so he closed them again. He slumped back on the grass. "I don't know who they were. I just need to be able to see again." Nasher lay on the grass and put his hands over his stinging eyes, forcing himself not to cry in front of Jamella. Then slowly, his rage began to rise.

Whoever did this to him would get a six-inch knife twisted deep into their chest. As Nasher lay on the grass, recovering from the ordeal he had just suffered, and Jamella remained silent as she sat next to him, there was only one thing coursing through his mind.

Violent murder.

Chapter Eleven
A dangerous escalation of violence
February 2008

The footage of Nasher rolling on the grassy field, wailing like a baby while being doused with milk, spread through the school like a common cold the next day. Although the footage was a little grainy, and Kwesi seemed unable to keep his hands still, you could tell that it was Nasher suffering in the video. By the time it was lunchtime, practically every pupil at Kingsland Academy, from year 7s right up to the sixth formers, had watched the footage on Facebook or viewed it on their phones. With the footage amassing 500 likes on Facebook by lunchtime and shared more than 350 times, Nasher's reputation at school as a feared roadman had been flipped on its head overnight.

"I beg you play it again," Carlos said, peering over Gavin's shoulder. "I need to laugh one more time, innit."

Gavin was sitting at the dinner table in the cafeteria. Huddled around him were Yemi, Kwesi, Andrew, Toby and Carlos. All of them were standing behind Gavin, looking over his shoulder. Gavin went into the folder in his phone where his videos were stored. He found the Nasher footage, selected it and pressed play. The boys snickered as they watched the footage for the umpteenth time. With each new viewing, Gavin noticed small details in how Nasher's legs thrashed about or how his tongue kept waggling like a dog as his face was buried in a stream of thick milk. After the 30-second footage ended, the boys sat back down.

Andrew looked around, ensuring no one in the cafeteria was paying them attention, and leaned forward towards Gavin. "Fam, I can't believe you man actually did that," he said in a hushed voice. "You got the whole school mocking Nasher. I never thought this day would come. You know you man are my heroes now, right?"

Gavin turned to Yemi, and they both grinned at each other. Kwesi, who was quietly eating his lunch, shook his head in disapproval. "He got what was coming to him. Karma, innit," Gavin said, raising his fist towards Yemi, who bashed his fist against Gavin's.

"Dun know," Yemi said with a satisfied nod. "Man thought just because we're in year 7, we were gonna take his abuse like some waste men. But who's the wasteman now, you get me. Sorry, I meant to say, who's the milkman now."

All of the boys burst into eye-watering laughter, all except Kwesi. After the boy's chortling had finished, Kwesi looked at Yemi and Gavin, who were both sitting opposite him. He looked apprehensive, like someone who knew victory did not last forever.

"We just better hope Nasher doesn't find out it was us," Kwesi said. "Because if he does, we'll have to move out of Hackney. Like today. I ain't even joking, you know."

"You overthink too much, Big K," Yemi said. He put his right hand reassuringly on Kwesi's shoulder. "There's no way Nasher's gonna find out. We were wearing masks. We're good, man."

"Yeah, don't stress yourself, Big K," Gavin said, smiling at Kwesi. "We pulled off the perfect revenge."

Kwesi let out a sigh. "If you man say so, innit," he said, sounding unconvinced.

******

When Nasher punched the brick wall at the back of the school, he felt the explosion of pain ripple through his right hand. And yet, he did not scream or even wince in agony. Standing around Nasher were his usual crew, watching him with concerned looks. Nasher stood facing his back towards them. He was breathing heavily after releasing all that rage against the inanimate concrete. The knuckles on his wrist had torn open, leaking blood. Nasher did not care. The anger tearing through him made everything numb.

"Yo fam, you good though?" K Dot said, his voice tiptoeing out of his mouth.

Nasher swung around and went straight for K Dot like an attack dog. He grabbed K Dot by his school blazer and pulled the scrawny Bengali boy towards his grimacing face. "Why would I be good right now? Why are you such a retard, man?"

K Dot was cowering now. "I am...I am…sorry, Nash—"

Before K Dot could finish saying Nasher's name, he slapped him so hard across the face that the bubble gum K Dot was chewing flew from his mouth like a bullet. Now whimpering, K Dot bowed his head. Nasher pushed him back to the rest of the group with brute force. If Harris had not grabbed K Dot, he would have fallen onto the floor, inflicting further damage on K Dot's already abysmal ratings among the gang. Although Nasher got some satisfaction from belittling K Dot, who was now rubbing his right cheek and looking like a sad puppy, Nasher's rage had not cooled.

Nina came to stand next to Nasher. She gently put her hand on his shoulder. "Bruv, we tried to find out where the video came from and who uploaded it on Facebook, but we don't know, innit. Everyone just started sharing it this morning as soon as school started."

Nasher clenched his right fist. Blood from his bruised knuckles trickled down onto the concrete floor. "I need to find out who rushed me, Nina." Nasher looked at her, both his fists now shaking. "When I find them man, they're dead. I am gonna bore them up differently." It was more than a threat. It was a deadly promise.

"Oi Nasher, remind me again," Harris said, stepping forward from the group. "Before them boys in the masks and bikes came, you was linking Jamella, alie?"

"Yeah, I told you that already, man," Nasher said, narrowing his eyes at Harris. He kissed his teeth. "What's your point, blud?"

"You don't think that's weird, nah?"

"What'd you mean?"

"I hear what Harris is saying," Nina interjected, nodding her head in contemplation. "Like, bruv, I don't get why she wanted to link you. It don't make sense. Why would any girl wanna link a man when that man dun cussed her out in a diss track?"

Nasher shrugged his shoulders. Girls were freaky, and sometimes they did things that had no logic when they were in their feelings for a guy. This is what his two older brothers had always told Nasher anyway. "I don't know, man," Nasher said, shaking his head at Nina. He was becoming very irritable. "Girls move mad, innit. You know your lot better than I do, you get me. Man's not got a vagina, have I?"

"Exactly," Nina said. "There's no way a chick is gonna just link a man that did her dirty the way you did, fam. There was another reason."

Nasher looked at Nina. "So what you telling me then?"

"She's saying that Jamella set you up, G," Harris said with a hint of impatience. "It was a honey trap ting, you get me."

Nasher's first reaction was outright refusing the possibility that Nina and Harris were right. But the more he thought about the circumstances in which Jamella had linked him, it started to feel suspicious. Her random texts on Sunday morning and being overly sexual so quickly over the text messages. Even when he met with Jamella at the park, she was dressed in a revealing way to make herself look like she was proper into him. It all felt a bit staged now that Nasher really thought about it. He could feel his heartbeat rise, and he clenched his teeth.

"Let's go chat to Jamella and really see wagwan with her. Who knows what class she had before lunch break?"

Nina gave Nasher a devilish grin. "One of my youngers is in her class. I can find out right now."

******

Playing with her Blackberry Curve, Jamella sat opposite Mabel on the work table. The science classroom was empty apart from the two of them. Mr Cleghorn, their sixty-year-old science teacher, had left them in the room to sort out an issue with another teacher in the staff room. While Mabel frowned, Jamella sat on the metal stool, dangling her legs and smiling as she typed the text she was going to send to Gavin.

"This is so long," Mabel said, folding her arms. She looked longingly out the window onto the playground outside where year 10 and year 11 boys were playing football and girls stood on the side lines, cheering them on. "I can't believe Mr Cleghorn gave us detention at lunchtime. He's such a wasteman with his yellow teeth that are desperately crying for a dentist appointment." Mabel kissed her teeth. When Jamella did not respond, she turned her head to face her best friend. "Oi, Rihanna, I am talking, you know," she said, shaking her head. "Can you stop messaging your boo for one minute, please."

Jamella looked up from her phone. She had just sent Gavin a text telling him how she could not wait to kiss him after school. She blinked at Mabel. "Sorry, I didn't hear what you said. What did you say?"

With an exaggerated eye roll, Mabel sighed and waved her right hand dismissively at Jamella. "Whatever, forget about it, gurl." She then started fidgeting and gave Jamella a bashful look. "Hey, could…could you ask Gavin if Yemi is gonna be with him after school?"

Jamella sniggered and grinned at her friend.

"What? Why are you smiling like that?" Mabel kissed her teeth again. "Have you got something stuck in your teeth?"

"When are you just gonna admit you like Yemi?" Jamella said with a smirk. "It's so obvious, you know.

"Gurl, I don't know what you're chatting about. I just wanna know if he's gonna be with Gavin after school so we can all hang out at Hackney Marshes together." Mabel shrugged her shoulders as if it was nothing more than that.

But Jamella could see right through her best friend like she was Casper. "Just ask him out."

Mabel scoffed as if what Jamella had suggested was the most outlandish thing she had ever heard. "Are you dumb? I don't ask boys out, innit. They ask me out."

"With that attitude, you're gonna be single forever like some of my aunties back in Barbados."

As they laughed together at Jamella's joke, there was a sudden loud and aggressive knock on the door. Both Jamella and Mabel sharply turned their head. Through the door's rectangular window, they saw Nina. She had a big grin, but it was anything but friendly. Before either could run to the door and lock it, it swung open.

Nina entered the science classroom. She was immediately followed by the rest of Nasher's goons. Wearing his signature black and grey New Era baseball cap, Nasher was the last to enter. Even when he smiled at Jamella and Mabel, there was a menacing undertone. The look Nasher gave her at that moment, full of venomous hatred, no one had ever given her. Jamella felt sweat on her armpits, and her breathing became heavier. Now she could feel her heart pounding.

"Wagwan, girls?" Nasher said, flashing the grills in his teeth. "Oi Skilla, shut the door and lock it." Skilla walked over to the classroom door. Jamella's heart filled with dread as she heard the door lock.

"Why are you looking so shook to see me?" Nasher said, taking slow and measured steps towards Jamella, his eyes locked onto her like a sniper's laser. He stopped a few steps away from the worktable. "Yesterday at the park you was bare quick to lipse man up, and now you're looking at me like I am about to kill you." Nasher chuckled, each laugh dripping with the promise of violence. His gang snickered behind him.

"I…I…didn't know you were gonna come here," Jamella stuttered, trying but knowing she was failing to keep her voice even. Nasher glanced at her Blackberry in front of her that she had stupidly put on the worktable. Realising her grave error, Jamella reached for her phone, but Nina had swiped it off the table in one rapid movement.

"Come on, Nina. You can't just go through my phone like that."

"Oi, shut up!" Nina said, throwing a fierce look of hatred at Jamella. "You pound shop Rihanna. You think you're so smart and peng. But you messed with the wrong people, you get me."

The feeling of dread sunk into Jamella's chest as Nina went through her phone, making her hands shake. She looked at the door when she thought of running out of the classroom. But Skilla was guarding the entrance. He saw Jamella look in his direction and gave her a grin, shaking his head at her as if to say, 'don't even think about it.'

"Bruv, come see these texts," Nina said, walking up to Nasher and showing him something on Jamella's Blackberry. Nasher looked at the phone while Nina held it to his face. "She's been texting Brixton boy. She's still linking my man." Nina threw Jamella's Blackberry on the floor and shot her a contemptuous look. "You wanna take us for *eediyat,* yeah? You light-skinned girls always think you're so sly. Until you get caught out."

Nasher's emotionless eyes rested on Jamella. Now she could feel her whole body shaking.

"You really did me dirty like this," Nasher said, feigning disappointment. He sighed as if he was about to regret his next action. "It's always the pretty girls you gotta put your hands on."

Jamella decided to take her chances. She leapt from her stool and dashed towards the door. She heard Mabel scream. Nasher quickly reacted and threw himself onto Jamella with his whole body weight, flooring her quickly. Jamella landed hard on the ground and felt the back of her head smack the floor.

As Jamella lay on the ground, moaning as her head throbbed with pain, she suddenly felt someone's huge, thick hands wrap around her neck. She opened her eyes to the sight of Nasher on top of her. His dark eyes were filled with crazed madness as he tightened his hands around her throat, his fingers digging into her neck.

"Who were the boys that rushed me at the park?"

Even if Jamella wanted to answer Nasher's question, she could not. Nasher's hands, which were heavy and hot, were crushing her throat. Air was not reaching her mouth. Desperate, Jamella slapped her hands against the floor and thrashed her feet. But Nasher kept strangling her.

"Nasher," Skilla said, his voice filled with horror, "bruv, she can't breathe!"

"Shut your mout' and guard the door!" Nasher roared back.

Jamella desperately kicked her legs and wiggled her body, but Nasher's grip was not loosening. Nasher continued to crush Jamella's oesophagus with his bare hands. Now she was barely taking in air and she could no longer breathe properly.

"You're going to kill her!" Mabel screamed, her voice piercing everyone's ears. "Stop, Nasher!"

"No!" Nasher roared, spit flying from his mouth. "Tell me who those boys were! I know you know who did it. Tell me!"

Jamella felt tears run down her cheeks as she gasped desperately for air and her life. Her vision was becoming blurry as her head started to spin. Was this what dying felt like?

"Ok, I'll tell you who did it. Just get off her!"

It was Mabel's voice. As soon as Nasher heard what Mabel said, he unclasped his hands from Jamella's neck.

In fits of coughing, Jamella took in a massive air intake, having been starved of it for what felt like minutes. She began to sob as she put her hands around her bruised neck.

Nasher stood up from the floor where Jamella lay in a fit of tears. Breathing heavily from all the strength he had used to strangle Jamella, he advanced towards Mabel. "So, who were the boys then?"

Mabel briefly glanced at Jamella. She was holding her bruised neck, which was now slightly disfigured with pinkish and purplish bruises. With tears sliding down her eyes, Jamella looked back at Mabel with fear.

"It was Gavin, Yemi and Kwesi, alright," Mabel finally said, shaking her head as she said it. "But Nasher, it was just a stupid joke, ok. Please don't do anything bad to them. I am begging you."

"Just a stupid joke?" Nasher said. To everyone's surprise in the room, Nasher let out a cackling laugh. He took three steps towards Mabel, and she took one step back, but Nina, standing behind Mabel, pushed her forward. Now Nasher was mere inches from her face; their foreheads practically touching.

From the ground, Jamella could see the terror in Mabel's eyes as her friend's legs began to wobble. Nasher stood in front of her with clenched fists.

"Do I look like the type of boy who likes to be part of a stupid joke?" Nasher said, never taking his eyes off Mabel. When Nasher was met with silence, he smirked. "That's what I thought." Without warning, Nasher gave Jamella a hard backhand on her left cheek. So powerful was the force of Nasher's hand that it almost sent Mabel flying across the room as she stumbled sideways and collapsed on the floor.

"Mabel!" Jamella shouted. Getting on her knees, she scurried over to her friend and shook her on the shoulder. Mabel began to stir and moan.

"After school, we're gonna ambush Brixton boy and those two little pricks he jams with," Nasher said, looking at his gang as he addressed them. He turned his attention to Nina. "I threw the shank over the gates at the back of the school. It should be in the bushes somewhere. Go and get that."

Nina nodded her head. "Say no more, fam. I'll go collect that now, innit." She hurried out of the classroom.

Jamella knelt on the floor, comforting Mabel as she was in too much shock to look up at Nasher, the first boy to ever physically attack her. But when Nasher spoke, she could hear his voice's cold and murderous tone all too clearly.

"You should never have chosen Brixton boy over me. Now I am gonna make him bleed out when I plunge my knife into his stomach and carve my man up."

Chapter Twelve

Run for your life

February 2008

The bell reverberated across the school.

Its loud, incessant ringing travelled through every corridor and every classroom. It even reached the mostly empty playground, save for a few truant pupils lingering at the back of the school, playing penny up the wall, smoking cigarettes or snogging. At the end of every school day, chairs were scraped back as students got up and packed books into their bags. Grateful for home time, many were no longer listening to the well-to-do teacher shouting over the chorus of voices. The overworked and underpaid teacher reminded his young pupils not to forget their homework and to read the chapter in a textbook that would be the focus of the next lesson. The teacher's words fell on deaf ears and distracted minds. Lockers were slammed shut as young minds collected their bags and hidden fags. Classroom doors swung open, and students poured out like a fountain of youth. The school day was over for today. But tomorrow, the discovery of the world and the evolution of oneself, the cycle of a teenager's life, would begin again, anew.

Side by side, Gavin and Yemi walked out of their geography class, laughing together in banter. They were sharing a joke about how Miss Rosalyn, their geography teacher, would go in red in the face when she struggled to pronounce any African surnames.

"Fam, I am telling you she butchers my surname all the time," Yemi said, grinning at Gavin as they walked down the noisy corridor filled with chattering students. "She's better off giving up and skipping me on the register because I feel embarrassed for her when she tries to say my last name."

Gavin chuckled. "But to be fair, fam, you have a proper *Af* surname, innit. I ain't gonna lie, I can't pronounce it, and I ain't gonna try to, you get me. You got one of those surnames where if you aren't born Nigerian, it's impossible for someone to say it properly."

Kwesi, passing through the crowd of students with his big frame, came towards them. He seemed to be in happier spirits compared to lunchtime. "What's good, you man?" he said, standing in front of Gavin and Yemi. "Kicking ball after school, yeah?"

"Nah, not this afternoon," Gavin said, tapping his left foot on the floor. "Linking Jamella later, innit. But man's definitely kicking ball tomorrow, for sure."

"Is Mabel gonna be with Jamella?" Yemi said, giving Gavin a side-eye.

Gavin kissed his teeth and shoved Yemi lightly on the shoulder. "You hearing this guy? Don't think I ain't pree you chirpsing her, Yemz."

Yemi shook his head, but a smile remained on his face. "Don't watch face, bruv. But if Mabel is gonna be with Jamella, then we might as well all jam together, you get me." Yemi turned back to Kwesi.

"I might miss footy as well, Big K. But tomorrow, man's there."

Kwesi grunted and put his left hand on his forehead as if he had a headache. "Why are you two so gassed over girls, man? All they do is suck time away from the real fun things in life."

Before Gavin could describe to Kwesi the sweet sensation of kissing a girl so he understood why girls were so addictive, his attention was diverted. Mabel was hurrying towards them. As she came closer, she had a look of panic on her face, and Gavin noticed her right eye looked slightly swollen. To Gavin and Kwesi's shock, Mabel threw herself onto Yemi, who looked just as perplexed. She began to sob.

"I am so sorry, Yemi. I am really sorry," she wept, burying her head into Yemi's chest.

Yemi stepped back and held Mabel by the shoulders. "Hey, what's wrong?" he said, looking at Gavin and Kwesi and then back at Mabel. "Where's Jamella? And what happened to your left eye?"

"It's Nasher," she said through gritted teeth.

"What? Nasher did that to your eye?" Yemi said, raising the base in his voice.

"Yeah, but it don't matter right now," Mabel said, panic returning to her face. "Him and his goons are coming for all of you. He knows it was you lot who rushed him at the park."

"What, how?" Gavin said, his heart already starting to pound faster. Kwesi moaned as if someone had just punched him in the stomach.

Mabel turned her head away from Yemi, Gavin and Kwesi. She looked at the floor. Her voice was unsteady. "Because I…I told him."

Gavin cocked his head back, Yemi gasped, and Kwesi widened his eyes.

"Why would you do that, man?" Gavin said, running his head through his braids.

"Because he was strangling your *girlfriend* in the classroom we were sitting in for detention," Mabel said sharply, whipping her head at Gavin and giving him a stern look.

"Hold up," Gavin said, shaking his head as he could not believe what he was hearing, "Nasher put his hands on Jamella?"

"Yes, Nasher and his goons came to the classroom where we were staying in for detention. Nina went through Jamela's phone, and when Nasher saw that Jamella was still texting you, he attacked Jamella." Mabel closed her eyes as if in agony and shook her head before continuing. "It looked like he was gonna kill her unless Jamella or me told him who rushed him at the park, innit." Tears started to creep at the edges of her eyes. "What else was I supposed to do? What if he actually killed her? What choice did I have?"

"It's ok, Mabel," Yemi said, pulling her into a tight embrace. She hugged Yemi back.

"Man, we're dead boys walking," Kwesi said, burying his whole head in his hands. "I told you man it was a bad idea to get revenge on him. Now Nasher is gonna kidnap us and kill us."

"Oi, will you relax, Big K," Gavin said, trying to sound like he was not worried when he was in fact panicking deep down. Gavin looked at Mabel, who was still in a tight hug with Yemi. "Where's Jamella now? Is she ok?" Gavin heard the fear mixed with anger in his voice. The thought of Jamella being strangled by Nasher's hands and he had not been there to defend her made him shake with fury.

"She's in the girl's toilets, but she's fine. But listen to me, yeah." Mabel removed herself from Yemi's arms and looked deep into Gavin's eyes. He saw terror staring right back at him. "Nasher and his gang are waiting for you lot outside the front gates," Mabel said, rubbing away her tears with the palms of her hands. "When you come out, they're gonna rush you and do a lot worse. You guys gotta escape from the back, so they don't clock you. I know a fire exit."

Gavin's mind felt frazzled and deeply stressed as he followed Mabel through the school's corridors. Yemi and Kwesi walked beside him, keeping the same hurried pace. Mabel led them into a deserted hallway that was so quiet they could hear their footsteps. She opened a grey door which led to a small, concrete room filled with mops, buckets, black bin bags and smelt of soap and dust. There was a white door at the end of the room.

"Go through that white door. It leads you to the car park," Mabel said. "Then run to the bus stop. I wouldn't risk walking home." She hugged Yemi and then nodded her head at Gavin and Kwesi. "Please be careful, guys. And just get home safe."

Gavin looked away from Mabel, suddenly feeling annoyed at her. Deep down, however, he knew his annoyance was not justified. What was he expecting Mabel to do? Not reveal who had ambushed Nasher and risk Jamella being seriously hurt or worse at the hands of that lunatic?

"Ok, you man, let's move quickly," Gavin said, nodding at Yemi and Kwesi.

Leaving Mabel behind, Gavin, Yemi and Kwesi bolted through the room towards the white door. When Gavin reached the door, he pushed it open by pressing his hands against the metal bar handle. Sunlight flooded Gavin's eyesight, and the sound of noisy Kingsland Academy students leaving school filled his ears.

Gavin peeped his head out and surveyed his surroundings. In front of him was the car park. It was located right at the back of the school. Now doing his best to concentrate and think, Gavin was unsure how they would get to Shacklewell Lane bus stop.

Yemi came to stand next to Gavin. "Bruv, we can cut through that street to get to the bus stop," he said, pointing his finger towards a residential street called Charterhouse Road, a couple of feet away. "But let's move quickly because we're wasting bare time, innit." Yemi turned back and looked at Kwesi. "You cool, Big K?"

Silently and with a solemn look, Kwesi nodded his head.

"Calm, let's do this."

The three boys scurried through the car park in a crouching position, their heads turning in every direction as if they were on a battlefield and bullets were whizzing above them. As soon as they had left the car park, Gavin, Yemi, and Kwesi dashed through Charterhouse Road, passing the brown-bricked low-rise flats, parked cars and street lamp posts.

They emerged onto Amhurst Road. It was busy with activity. Cars were speeding by on the main road in front of them. Many Kingsland Academy students were walking on the pedestrian pavement in groups. The Shacklewell Lane bus stop was three minutes up the road.

"Ok, I think we're good," Yemi said, looking around.

"The bus stop is that way, yeah?" Gavin said, pointing up the road.

"Yeah," Kwesi said, who was unable to keep still, his eyes darting in every direction.

"Alright, let's go," Gavin said, who had already started walking up the road. "We're bare lucky, you know. Mabel just saved our asses, to be fair to her."

But Gavin had claimed good fortune prematurely. From some distance behind him, he heard the last voice in the world that he wanted to hear.

"Oi, I see them over there!" Nasher bellowed from down the road.

Gavin turned around and felt fear jolt through him. Nasher and the rest of his gang were sprinting towards them. A 15-inch Rambo knife flashed in Nasher's hand as sunlight bounced off its stainless steel blade.

"Run!" Gavin screamed.

Propelled by adrenaline and pure fear, Gavin, Yemi and Kwesi sprinted up Amhurst road. Gavin did not dare look back but kept running forward, his heart racing and breathing fast and heavy. From behind him, Gavin could hear many feet hitting the concrete pavement.

"Stop running you pussyholes!" came Nasher's loud and aggressive voice from behind which felt dangerously close and Gavin realised Nasher and his goons were catching up fast.

Up ahead, the 276 bus could be seen in the distance. It looked like the bus was two minutes away from Shacklewell Lane bus stop, which came into Gavin's periphery, shrouded by a tall tree.

"If we wait at the bus stop, Nasher is gonna catch up to us," Gavin shouted back at Yemi and Kwesi. He quickly spun his head back. Nasher and his goons had gained significant ground. Nasher's eyes were filled with a frightening amount of murderous intent. That was enough for Gavin to summon extra energy reserves and launch himself forward. He bolted past the bus stop, Yemi and Kwesi trailing behind by a few precious seconds, and ran to the front of the bus before it reached the bus stop.

Gavin banged on the bus's front door and shouted. The bus driver, a middle aged black woman wearing a headscarf and oddly reminding Gavin of his mum, opened the door. Never in his life had Gavin felt so much relief wash over his soul.

As soon the bus door's opened, Gavin, Yemi and Kwesi almost tumbled into the bus. Quickly regaining his footing, Gavin pressed his hands against the plastic window that separated passengers from the bus driver's compartment. "Please, miss.

We're being chased by some people. Can you just drive and not stop at the next bus stop?"

The bus driver looked at her windshield and could also see the gang of pupils in school uniform sprinting towards the bus, and they would reach it within a few seconds. Maybe she would have ignored Gavin's request, but she must have seen the blade that Nasher was brandishing. Just as Nasher and his gang reached the bus, she closed the front passenger door. Nasher banged his fists against the bus door, and Gavin heard him scream as the bus drove away. The bus driver did not stop at Shacklewell Lane bus stop.

Gavin, Yemi and Kwesi leaned against the yellow metal bar attached to the wall for people to hold as the bus moved. All three of them were panting, desperately catching their breaths. "Thank you," Gavin said to the bus driver. She did not acknowledge him and continued facing the windshield as she drove the bus down Amhurst road.

"We did it, man," Gavin said, slapping Yemi on the shoulder and nodding his head at Kwesi. "Fam, that was too close."

Yemi shook his head and looked at Gavin. Horror stretched across his face like a long shadow, and his mouth trembled. "Oi, you man, I just remembered something."

"What?" Kwesi said, looking at Yemi, frightened.

"Nasher knows where we live."

******

Nasher banged his fists against the bus door, but the bus driver did not open it. Instead, she drove the bus down Amhurst road, failing to stop at the next bus stop. Nasher gripped his Rambo knife, roared into the street and stabbed at the air to vent his frustration. Then a thought quickly entered his mind as Nasher remembered a crucial piece of information.

Concealing his Rambo knife inside his school trousers, Nasher turned to his crew. They looked at him with expectant faces.

"What'd we do now, fam?" Nina said.

"You lot go to the studio. I'll link you later, innit. I'll finish this, don't worry."

"You sure, cuz?" Harris.

"Yeah, man," Nasher said, giving Harris a menacing look. "Why do I always gotta repeat myself? I said I will finish this, innit. I'll link you lot later."

"Ok, say no more, G," Nina said, nodding her head.

Nasher bashed his fists against each one of his loyal gang members and watched as they boarded a bus heading towards Hoxton. As the bus sped away, Nasher retrieved his phone from his pocket and scrolled through his contacts. Finding the person he wanted to call, Nasher dialled their number. He placed the phone by his right ear as it rang.

"What you telling me?" said Tunde Ogbodo, Nasher's older brother, from the other end of the line. "Did you get them yutes, yeah?"

"Nah, they legged it, but I know where they live, innit."

"Calm. Where's that?"

"Pembury Estate, still."

"Say no more," Tunde said. "Auntie lives there, and those Pembury Boys ain't gonna say nothing to us if we turn up in their manor anyway. I know them man. Where are you now?"

"On Amhurst road."

"Good. I am one minute away, and I am with Bola, innit. We'll come pick you up and drive straight to the estate."

Chapter Thirteen
The Notorious Nash Twins

February 2008

As soon as they reached Hackney Downs Station, Gavin, Kwesi, and Yemi quickly alighted the bus. Gavin's heartbeat had not slowed since Nasher and his gang had chased them. The deadly dagger that Nasher held in his hand flashed in Gavin's mind, and he remembered Jamal's life had been snatched away from him by an almost identical knife. The thought of it made Gavin want to throw up, but he composed himself. As he walked briskly across the street towards the traffic junction, Yemi and Kwesi by his side, his mind was racing. *What do we do now?*

"Oi, I think we should go to my uncle's," Gavin said, looking at both sides of the junction before crossing. Pembury road was on the adjacent street. "He will know what to do, innit."

"Your uncle? What the barber?" Kwesi said, raising his eyebrows at Gavin. "Why would he know what to do in this situation, man?"

"I don't know, Big K. But what else are we gonna do? Are you man really gonna tell your parents about this?"

"Nah, allow that," Yemi said. "My mum and dad will go crazy. Probably ship me to Nigeria if I told them what's going on."

"I'll be on the 8am flight to Ghana. Economy as well," Kwesi added.

Briefly forgetting their life-threatening situation, Gavin laughed alongside Yemi and Gavin as they walked up Pembury road towards Pembury estate. The enclosure was empty when they reached their part of the estate. None of the Pembury boys who hung around the estate were around. Gavin's heart sank a little as he was hoping maybe the gang members who lived and hung around the estate would protect them from Nasher, and he would not have to get his uncle involved.

Accepting that no one would help them, Gavin turned to Yemi and Kwesi, standing next to each other. "Alright, you man, let's head over to my uncle's."

Before Gavin, Yemi and Kwesi could start making their way to uncle Reece's flat, a silver Mercedes C Class screeched into the enclosure and sped towards the boys. Gavin, Yemi and Kwesi threw themselves out of the way of the speeding vehicle. The Mercedes came to a grinding halt, blocking the path to Crandale house.

Gavin, Yemi, and Kwesi regained their footing and hurried to stand next to each other. They watched three people step out of the Mercedes that had nearly run them over. First, there was Nasher, still gripping the sinister blade in his hand as he stepped out of the backseat. From the driver's side, a muscular, six-foot-tall black man wearing a blue durag and a red and white, leather Avirex jacket came out of the driver's door. Then, another equally well-built and tall black man stepped out from the passenger's door. He wore a brown New Era hat, a denim jacket and jeans with brown Timberland boots.

"It's the Nash twins," Kwesi said, his soft voice thick with dread.

"Oi, where are you youngers going?" Nasher said, raising the blade as he walked towards the boys. "You're in deep shit, now." He smiled, flashing his grills.

Gavin quickly looked at Kwesi and Yemi. "We gotta run!"

"Oh no, you don't, you pricks!"

The chase began again.

Gavin, Yemi and Kwesi bolted through the estate with Nasher hot on their trails.

"We need to split up!" Gavin yelled, propelling himself forward.

"No!" Kwesi shouted, slightly behind Gavin and Yemi, as he struggled to keep up.

"Do it!"

Kwesi darted off to the right, Yemi sprinted to the left, and Gavin continued to pelt it forward. He looked back and saw that Nasher had chosen to go after him. There was no sign of the Nash twins. Increasing his pace, Gavin saw black railings ahead that surrounded a small courtyard.

"When I get you, you're dead, blud!" Nasher shouted from behind him. He was too close.

Gavin leapt over the black railings but lost his footing. He slammed his face against the grass and rolled forward on the ground. But Gavin quickly got to his feet, but Nasher jumped over the railings, landing neatly into the courtyard without stumbling.

Like two cowboys in a standoff, Gavin and Nasher now circled each other in the courtyard. Gavin could have kept running, but he knew there was no point as Nasher was too close now. The silver blade gleamed in Nasher's hands. Sweat dripped down Gavin's brow, and he trembled as he kept glancing at Nasher's knife. If that blade went inside Gavin, it would be the end of his life.

"You pussyhole," Nasher spat. "I told you before this ain't south, innit. You should have listened, Brixton boy. Us Hackney man don't play around, and now you about to find out what happens when you mess with us." Nasher tightened his grip on the blade, ready to lunge at Gavin with it.

Then Gavin looked over Nasher's shoulders to see Yemi jump over the railings. He threw a small stone at the back of Nasher's head.

"Arrgh!" Nasher screamed, stumbling forward as he rubbed the back of his head where the stone had connected.

"Run!" Yemi screamed.

Gavin did not need telling twice and followed Yemi as they both vaulted over the railings, leaving the courtyard. As they entered another enclosure in the great maze of Pembury estate, the silver Mercedes from earlier came screeching in front of them. The two muscular twins exited the car and ran towards them. Gavin and Yemi stopped dead in their tracks.

No matter how fast Gavin and Yemi were, they would not outrun two grown men. Even as the two turned on their heels to sprint, the two Nash twins were already upon them. One of the twins grabbed

Gavin by the neck and immediately had him in a headlock. The other Nash twin had done the same to Yemi.

"Stop struggling, likkle man," said the Nash Twin whose huge biceps were crushing Gavin's neck. "It's only going to get worse. You was big enough to do what you did, so now you and your boy over there can take the punishment like big men."

"Please let me go," Yemi cried. "Please."

"Nah, don't start with no waterworks," the other Nash twin said as Yemi struggled but failed to break the headlock he was in. "You boys knew what you were doing. These are the consequences, you get me."

In front of him, Gavin saw Nasher come and stand before them. There was a wicked grin stretched across his face. Like a butcher ready to slice up some meat, Nasher raised his blade forward, pointing it directly at Gavin. He took a few steps forward and then stopped, standing five or six steps away from Gavin.

"You're dead, Brixton boy," Nasher said, his silver grills reflecting light so his wicked smirk was partially blinding. "You're a dead man, blud."

Gavin closed his eyes and felt hot tears trickle down his cheeks. *Look what I've done.* He was about to be stabbed, and maybe Yemi too. If he had heeded Kwesi's warnings, he would not have ended up in this situation. Realising how close he was to his potential death, Gavin's mind jumped to thoughts of his mum. If he died, what would that do to her? How could he let her go through such a thing? What about Mabel? How would she feel about his death? More tears gushed from Gavin's eyes, and snot came out of his nose. Lastly, he thought about Jamal. They had started primary school together. Played football and basketball together. Chased girls in the playground together. And now Gavin would be killed the same way Jamal had been - by the sharp edge of a blade.

"What do you think you're doing!?"

Gavin snapped his eyes open. At first, he thought he had imagined the voice, but he had not. Uncle

Reece stood behind Nasher, with Kwesi standing next to him who was trembling with fear and with teary eyes. Uncle Reece clutched a metal baseball bat in his right hand. He legitimately looked like someone capable of serious violence as he stared fiercely at Nasher. Gavin had never seen his uncle in this light before.

Nasher turned around you. He raised his blade at uncle Reece. "Who are you, blud?"

Uncle Reece swayed the baseball bat by his side. "Watch who you're talking to, Nelson. I still remember when you were a five-year-old running around your mum's house with a Power Ranger toy in your hand instead of a knife."

"Who is this prick talking to, bruv?" Nasher said, spitting on the floor. How do you know man's name, and did I say you could chat my name out?" Nasher made a stabbing motion with the blade towards uncle Reece who did not flinch.

"Ratchet…is that you?" said the Nash twin that had Gavin in a headlock.

"Yeah, it's me. Good to see you, Tunde," uncle Reece said, smiling. He then looked at the other Nash twin, who was holding Yemi. "It's been a long time, Bola."

"Yeah…it has," Bola replied with a flat tone.

Ratchet? Gavin had quickly gone from being scared he was about to be stabbed to death to total confusion. How did uncle Reece know the Nash twins, and why did they call him Ratchet? Nothing was making sense right now.

"How's your mum?" uncle Reece continued, in a tone so casual it was like he was having a conversation at a restaurant with old acquaintances.

"Yeah, she's bless. She's in good health," Tunde said impatiently. "But let's allow all this small talk, bruv. Why are you here and holding a baseball bat? Do you know these *yutes* or something?"

"Yeah, as a matter of fact, I do," uncle Reece said. He nodded his head at Gavin. "The boy whose neck you're about to snap is my nephew. And the boy that Bola is gripsing is my nephew's friend. Same with this boy standing next to me."

"Your nephew, yeah?" Tunde said with a slight chuckle. Despite being aware of Gavin's relation to uncle Reece, Tunde had not loosened his grip around Gavin's head. "Well, guess what, Ratchet, your nephew and his mates have been very disrespectful to my little brother. So there's gotta be punishment for that disrespect. You feel me? You know how it goes."

Reece had a thoughtful expression on his face as he nodded his head. He looked like he was thinking very carefully before he responded. "I hear that, but what exactly is this punishment going to be, Tunde? Are you gonna wet up my nephew and his friends, huh? Like, what is that going to do, really? Do you think David would have approved of that?"

The mention of the name 'David' seemed to enrage Nelson. He waved his blade in front of uncle Reece again. "How do you know about my brother David?" he said, an unexpected vulnerability in his tone. "Yo, who is this guy? I'll bore him now, you know."

"Shut up, Nelson," Bola commanded in a firm voice. "Show some respect. That's one of your *olders*, do you understand? And put the shank down."

Nasher turned to look at his older brother. To Gavin's utter disbelief, Nasher actually obeyed someone else. He slowly dropped his arm, holding the Rambo knife to his side.

"Nah, David wouldn't have approved," Tunde continued. "But still, I can't just allow this disrespect to go unpunished."

"Of course, it can't, and I never said it will," uncle Reece said. "I'll speak to my nephew and his friends. They will tell me what they've done, and I will make sure they show no more disrespect to your brother. How does that sound?"

Tunde hummed and went completely silent. Finally, after what felt like a long time, he spoke. "Because we've got history, and you did a lot for me back in the day, I am gonna say yes to what you've put forward. But know this, if you was anyone else, I wouldn't be this *lenient*. If your nephew and his boys disrespect my brother again, I won't show the same mercy as I did today."

"I know that very well, Tunde, so I am grateful. And believe me, the disrespect ends today."

"Nah, bun that!" Nasher shouted, waving the blade again. "These youngers have taken the absolute piss. I ain't having it. They ain't getting away with it. No way!"

"Why are you shouting?" Tunde said in a sharp tone that immediately sucked the hype and bravado from Nasher like a vacuum cleaner. "I have just said that this is how it will end. Don't you ever question my decisions again. Do I make myself clear, little brother?"

Nasher bowed his head. "Sorry, big bro. It won't happen again," he said in the tone of a child being chastised by his dad. Gavin's jaw almost dropped.

"Good, get in the car, innit. We're going back to the yard."

Tunde released Gavin from his headlock, and Bola did the same with Yemi. Rubbing his neck,

Gavin walked over to stand by his uncle, and Yemi went to stand by Kwesi.

The Nash twins walked back to their Mercedes. Nelson dragged himself behind his two older brothers, looking like a petulant child that had been denied a Christmas gift. Nasher and Bola got into the Mercedes, but as Tunde opened the driver's door, he turned back and looked at uncle Reece. There was a surprisingly warm smile on his face.

"I would have preferred better circumstances than this, but it's good seeing you again, Ratchet."

"Same here, man. Say hi to your mum for me," uncle Reece said, giving Tunde a brotherly smile. "Oh, and I opened up a barbershop on Mare street. You should pass through one time. I'll give you a trim, and we can laugh about the old days and trade stories about the notorious nineties."

"Yeah, I heard you started a barbershop business. I might have to take you up on that offer, bruv. Stay bless, Ratchet." With that, Tunde entered Mercedes. Its engine rumbled to life, and the Mercedes sped off, doing a sharp turn before screeching out of the estate, disappearing out of sight as it drove onto Pembury road.

Uncle Reece let out a deep sigh, and his shoulders relaxed. There were droplets of sweats running down the side of his face. It was only then that Gavin realised just how frightened uncle Reece had been during the whole exchange with Nasher's older brothers. How had his uncle managed to remain so calm and collected? He turned to Gavin.

"Nephew, you've got a lot of explaining to do," uncle Reece said, his voice serious. He then looked at Yemi and Kwesi. "You two better go home. Right now. Count yourselves very lucky. Today could have ended very differently."

Yemi and Kwesi looked up at uncle Reece as if he was their sensei and nodded. Then they both turned to Gavin and gave him a weak smile before scurrying away to their parents' flats in Crandale House.

"Let's go," uncle Reece said, putting his right hand on Gavin's back as he held the metal baseball bat with his left. "Looks like we've got a lot to chat about."

Chapter Fourteen
Role models

February 2008

Gavin took the hot mug filled with tea from uncle Reece. He was sitting on the brown sofa in the flat's living room. Even though the ordeal with Nasher and his brothers was over, Gavin was still shaking. Never in his life had he come so close to his own death.

Holding a mug as well, uncle Reece sat down next to Gavin. He took a sip of his tea and then looked at Gavin. There was a blank look on his face, and Gavin could not quite tell what his uncle was thinking. Until he was addressed, Gavin decided it was best he did not open his mouth.

"Ok, nephew. Start from the beginning," uncle Reece said. "I want to understand how you ended up getting involved with those two men. And don't lie to me about anything. Understand?"

Gavin nodded silently and began to tell the whole story. He told uncle Reece everything, from Nasher's jealousy and bullying towards Gavin because he was going out with Jamella all the way to the ambush at the park.

After Gavin explained his very eventful first month and a half living in Hackney, he took a long sip of his tea. Uncle Reece was quiet for a long time, and he had a look of deep contemplation on his face. Gavin became anxious as the silence stretched.

Finally, uncle Reece spoke. "You've been incredibly foolish, Gavin," he said, throwing Gavin a piercing look of disappointment. "Do you realise the danger you put yourself in? If your friend, Kwesi, had not knocked on my door in time and told me you were in trouble, you would not be sitting here next to me drinking PG tips tea. Instead, I would be on the phone with your mum, telling her that her only child, whom she had entrusted into my care, was bleeding to death in Homerton hospital. And why? Because he'd been stabbed. How would your mum feel about that? How would I feel about that? You even put your friends in life-threatening danger too. How would their parents have felt knowing one of their children had been stabbed to death all because you wanted revenge over some petty disrespect?"

Uncle Reece's words were like whips lashing on Gavin's guilt. He could now fully see that getting revenge on Nasher had made the whole situation between the two of them even worse. Nasher had almost strangled Jamella to death, and this was partly Gavin's fault because he had got her involved in his thirst to get even. Yemi could have been killed in the same way Jamal had died. Another best friend becoming a victim of the blade. Gavin put his mug on the wooden table in front of him. He burst into a sob.

"I am sorry, uncle Reece," Gavin wept, blinding tears running down his face. "I didn't know all of this was gonna happen." The shame of what he had done overwhelmed him, and he buried his head in his hands. "I am sorry. Please don't hate me."

"What?" uncle Reece said in a shocked tone. He sighed and placed his hand on Gavin's left shoulder. "I don't hate you. How can I hate the only nephew I have?" Uncle Reece's voice had taken on a softer tone. "But you need to start thinking about how you react to things, nephew. I know you feel angry when someone disrespects you, and I would too, but sometimes if you retaliate, you will only make things worse. This is one reason why we have black boys dying on London's streets, killed by other black boys. Black mothers are burying their children because of petty disrespect. It's never worth it, Gavin. Trust me."

"But what do I do then when someone is bullying me at school, uncle Reece?" Gavin said, his vision blurred with tears as he removed his face from his hands.

"You come and speak to me, and then I can speak to your teachers or whoever is bullying you; I can speak to their parents. But when you take matters into your own hands, well… you've seen what happens."

Gavin nodded and wiped his tears with his shirt sleeve.

Uncle Reece took another sip of his tea. "Gavin, it's very important to me that you don't end up a statistic. Not just as a victim of knife crime but as a victim of this road life claiming you young boys. I want you to be better than my generation of black boys growing up in London. Many of us got dragged into a criminal life, mainly because of our circumstances. I don't want that for you."

"Is that why you know the Nash twins, then?" Gavin asked, facing his uncle. "Were you a roadman before, and that's why they called you Ratchet? Was that your street name?"

At first, Gavin immediately regretted being so forward, thinking uncle Reece would be annoyed. But his uncle smiled at him, and then he turned his head to the window, looking out into the estate. There was a look on his uncle's face that Gavin could not quite read, but it seemed like his uncle was looking back into his past and digging out old memories.

"I was around sixteen years old when my dad, your grandad, died of an illness leaving just me, your mum and your grandma living in our flat in Brixton on Railton road," uncle Reece said. Even as he spoke, he remained fixed on the window. "I didn't handle my dad's death well and started acting up. I was getting into fights at college and getting into trouble with the police for dumb things like stealing chocolate bars and parker pens." Uncle Reece chuckled. "I went from being the best son in the world to the worst son you could imagine."

Gavin sat entirely still, fascinated by this past history his uncle Reece was sharing with him. There was a lot more to his uncle than he thought.

"I think I must have turned 18 when I got into a fight at a house party in Streatham with some boy from Lewisham," uncle Reece continued. "I remember knocking the boy out and feeling pretty chuffed with myself. But it turned out the boy I had decked was part of a big gang in Lewisham called the Ghetto Boys, and they were now after me. These guys were serious, and I couldn't put your

mum, you were in her belly then, and your grandma
in danger. So to avoid any drama, I left Brixton and
came to start afresh in Hackney."

Uncle Reece now turned to look at Gavin and
gave him a smile. "As you can see, we have a
similar story, nephew. Both of us are south
Londoners who moved to Hackney to escape
violence, only for violence to find us over here
anyway."

Gavin nodded silently, not sure what to say to
that. The tea in his mug was getting colder, but
Gavin no longer cared. He wanted to know the rest
of his uncle's story.

"So when I moved to Hackney, I first lived in
Fields Estate in London Fields," uncle Reece said.
"I soon got a job as a self-employed mechanic
fixing cars at a garage in Hoxton, and that's when I
met the Nash twins, Tunde and Bola. They were
actually older than me by three years, but they had a
younger brother my age named David. Nelson, or
Nasher as he calls himself now, was only a two-
year-old baby back then. But anyway, David and I

became proper bredrins. David was a good guy, man. A very religious and humble person."

As he took a deep breath, uncle Reece looked like he was becoming emotional. Gavin could tell this David guy brought up something painful in his uncle's past.

"Tunde and Bola were the complete opposite of David. The twins were part of a big gang in London Fields called the Nash Town Massive. Back in those days, we're talking the early to late 90s; they were proper notorious. They carried out violent robberies in Hackney, Newham and even as far as Tottenham, where they had a deadly feud with a gang from that area. But being a young black boy who couldn't deal with the trauma of his dad's death, I became attracted to the Nash twins' lifestyle. They drove the sport cars, bought bottles in the clubs and had women throwing themselves at them."

"So…you joined the Nash Town Massive?" Gavin said.

Uncle Reece nodded his head. "Yeah, I did when I was around 20 years old. To your mum and grandma, I was their sweet son and younger brother who had turned a new leaf in Hackney. But I never told them about my life as a gang member, whose nickname was Ratchet, because I was good at fixing cars and driving. It wasn't long before I became the getaway driver for the gang whenever they carried out a robbery or beat up someone who owed them money. It felt good to be part of a group of boys I looked up to at the time. Bless him, David would always warn me not to hang out with his brothers. He just went to college, got good grades and looked after their mum since their dad wasn't around."

"What happened to David?" Gavin asked.

Uncle Reece sighed and rubbed his eyes, and for a moment, Gavin wondered if his uncle was going to cry. "A couple of years later, I must have been around 25 at this point, and I'd been with the Nash Town Massive for a good few years now. I was at a nightclub called Palace Pavilion on Lower Clapton road. It's since closed down now. Anyway, I was celebrating David's 25th birthday at this nightclub. The Nash Twins were with me, as were most of the

Nash Town crew. We did not know that a couple of boys from Tottenham had pulled up to the venue. They were looking to get revenge because one of their people had been violently robbed by someone from the Nash Town Massive earlier that day. They fired shots as soon as they entered the venue and saw us."

Gavin watched uncle Reece close his eyes. He massaged his forehead and shook his head. "You ok, uncle Reece?"

"Yeah, I am good," uncle Reece said, regaining composure. "So, as I was saying, these gang members from Tottenham started shooting up the venue. God was watching over me because I managed to not get hit, but David… wasn't so lucky. A stray bullet entered his neck, and he died in the arms of his two older brothers. I remember watching David take his last breaths." Uncle Reece chuckled, but there was no humour in it. "And you know what the cruellest part about all of it? David was the only one killed that night, on his birthday, and he wasn't even about that gang life. He was studying to be a doctor at the time."

"So you watched your best friend die just like I did," Gavin said, feeling a lump in his throat.

"Yeah, that's right, nephew," uncle Reece said, looking at Gavin. His uncle's eyes were on the verge of tears, but none emerged. "After David was buried, I left the gang and went back to college to study business administration. I received a big chunk of money from a family member back in Jamaica and used that money to open up my barbershop. And I haven't looked back since. It took my friend being killed to turn me into a better man."

Uncle Reece moved closer to Gavin on the sofa and put his arms around him. It was the first time they had been so close to each other. "I am a better man now, and that's why I can be a good role model for you, Gavin. Your mum brought you here to live with me because she knows I will show you the right path. The Nash twins didn't learn from their brother's death, and sadly, Nasher will be led down the wrong path by his older brothers. You can see it's already happening. But that's not going to be you, Gavin. You won't end up dead or in prison because you have good people around you. Nasher doesn't."

As he nodded, Gavin felt warm tears trickle from the edges of his eyes again. Uncle Reece brought Gavin close to his chest and hugged him for the first time. He then stood from the sofa and looked down at Gavin. The no-nonsense look he often gave Gavin when speaking to him had now returned.

"Anyway, you're grounded because you lied to me about where you were going on Sunday and for all the trouble you have caused. And it's for a whole three months. Whilst you are grounded, I want you back home by 5pm, after school and no PlayStation either while your grounded. Oh, and nephew, promise me that you and your friends will stay away from Nelson from now on and do nothing to him. Sorry, I can't keep calling him Nasher. It's a stupid name."

Gavin had to stop himself from laughing at his uncle's jibe at Nasher. He nodded at uncle Reece. "I promise, uncle Reece. I ain't causing any more trouble."

"Good. Go upstairs, clean yourself up and get some rest. It's been a long day. For everyone."

Gavin stood from the sofa, picked up his school bag from the floor and made his way to his room. As he walked up the flight of stairs, he looked over the banister. Uncle Reece was now sitting down on the sofa again. He was looking out of the window in silence.

"Hey, uncle Reece," Gavin said, standing in the middle of the staircase.

Uncle Reece turned around and looked at Gavin from the sofa. "Yes, nephew?"

Gavin gave his uncle a genuine smile for the first time since moving in with him. "I just wanted to thank you for letting me live with you. I don't miss my dad when I am here because you're the best replacement I could have asked for."

Either uncle Reece was really good at holding back tears, or maybe he did not want Gavin to see him cry. "Get some sleep," he said softly and quickly turned his head away.

Beginning to feel the whole strain of the day's events weigh down on his body and mind, Gavin climbed the rest of the stairs and could not wait to collapse onto his bed and fall into a deep sleep.

Chapter Fifteen
Saying goodbye
February 2008

Gavin chewed on the soggy chip.

As always, the cafeteria was booming with students during lunchtime. Gavin sat at the dining table with Yemi, Kwesi, Andrew, Toby and Carlos. All of them were eating another dreadful lunch. Yemi, seated next to Gavin, bit into his hamburger and grimaced as he chewed. Kwesi was talking animatedly with Andrew, Toby and Carlos about Arsenal's upcoming FA cup game with Man Utd on the weekend. Despite all the noise and chatter swirling around him, Gavin was deep in his thoughts. Although it had now been a whole week since the ordeal with Nasher and the Nash twins, he kept thinking about uncle Reece's story, what happened with Nasher and what Jamella had gone through.

"Oi Gavin. Gavin? Hey, fam!" Kwesi said, poking him on the shoulder.

Gavin shook his head, taking himself out of his thoughts. He looked at Kwesi, who was giving him a concerned look.

"Everything bless?" Kwesi said. "It ain't like you to be bare quiet when we're chatting about Arsenal. Where's that big mouth?" Kwesi chuckled and grinned at Gavin.

"Yeah, I know," Gavin said, smiling back. "Man's just thinking about stuff, innit."

"The whole madness with the Nash twins?" Carlos said, eyeing Gavin. "It's still crazy that they chased you, Yemi and Big K through your estate. Gavz, real talks, how have you only been in Hackney for less than two months, and you've already got into beef with two of the most feared roadman in the ends? Yeah, you man from south are definitely trouble."

Gavin laughed and winked at Carlos. "Or maybe Hackney is just trouble, innit."

As the boys laughed at Gavin's remark, Yemi tapped Gavin's shoulder. "Oi, look who it is," he said.

Gavin looked across the cafeteria. Nasher was marching through the dining hall with his usual goons and Nina, his lieutenant, by his side. There was a skinny ginger boy, who was in year 8, standing in Nasher's path. Since the boy was speaking to his friends, he had not noticed Nasher coming towards him, so he did not step out of the way. Nasher pushed the boy out of his path with force. The year 8 boy stumbled forward and fell on the floor.

As Nasher approached the dining table that Gavin was sitting on, Gavin grew anxious. Was Nasher going to continue troubling him again, even after his older brothers had told him to squash the beef he had with Gavin and his friends?

Gavin and the boys stopped talking as Nasher stood in front of their dining table. His whole gang glared at them, and Nina had a look of disgust plastered on her face as she scanned each of their faces.

"You good, yeah?" Nasher said in a gruff voice, staring at Gavin.

Gavin looked up at Nasher and shrugged his shoulders. "Yeah, I am good."

"Cool."

And that was the end of the entire exchange. Nasher turned his head to Nina, nodded at her, and continued walking through the cafeteria, heading to the exit. As each member of Nasher's crew followed their leader, they gave Gavin and his friends filthy looks as they walked past, but none of them said anything. After Nasher and his goons had left the cafeteria, Gavin breathed a sigh of relief, as did the rest of the boys.

"Man, that was intense," Yemi said, looking at Gavin. "I really thought he was gonna try something."

"We don't need to worry about him anymore, you get me," Gavin said, smiling at Yemi and Kwesi. "Anyway, let's talk about this FA cup match." Gavin was now in a cheerier mood. "Big K, I bet you five pounds, yeah, that Arsenal is gonna thrash Man Utd this weekend. Fàbregas is scoring a hat trick."

******

On a chilly afternoon, with a faint wind in the air and the sky a cloudless blue, Gavin walked through the grassy field with Jamella. They had met up after school as they often did to go to Hackney Marshes. A couple of boys played football on the grassy field, shouting and screaming passionately as they played what looked like a very physical game of football. Gavin watched as one boy slide-tackled one of the strikers, sending him crashing and rolling on the ground in agony.

Jamella, who was usually always bubbly and talkative, was quiet as he walked beside her. Since Nasher had attached her, Jamella had not been the same girl. It was like Nasher had squeezed all the happiness and innocence from her that day he had strangled her. Some days, it made Gavin clench his fists in rage when he thought about it, and he wanted to get revenge on Nasher again. But he had promised uncle Reece he would not retaliate. Also, he did not want to make things worse again, especially after barely escaping with his life in his last encounter with Nasher and his two older, twin brothers.

Holding hands, Gavin and Jamella walked to their usual, secluded spot among the bushes. Gavin could hear the sounds of birds chirping, and he listened to a splash as someone threw something into the river a few feet ahead of them.

Jamella sat on a long, thick log and put her hands on her black skirt. Gavin sat next to her. She still wasn't smiling, and he noticed the bruises around her neck, not for the first time. Finally, Jamella turned to look at Gavin and gave him a weak smile.

"How are you feeling, baby?" Jamella asked, squeezing Gavin's hand gently.

"Yeah, I am good. What about you?"

"Not so good," Jamella replied in a faint voice. She rubbed her bruised neck with her free hand. "Ever since…Nasher did what he did to me, I am always scared, Gavin. I don't go to many classes anymore and if I do, I wear a scarf because I don't want people to see the bruises. When I am walking through the school corridors, I always look around every corner to make sure Nasher's not coming. Today, I saw him walking down the same hallway as me, and I rushed to the girl's toilets with Mabel, hid there and cried. Mabel is really tough; she doesn't even care about what he did to her. But I am not as strong as her."

Gavin caressed Jamella's hand. "Nah, don't say that. You are strong."

Jamella shook her head. "I didn't grow up in London. I don't have that rude girl toughness these Hackney girls have. I am just an island girl from the Caribbean." Jamella sighed and shook her head in frustration. "And I know if I report what Nasher did to me, it might make things worse, and I am too scared to risk it. So I have to leave the school."

Tears appeared at the edges of her eyes. "I can't stay at Kingsland Academy anymore, Gavin. I am too scared of him. Every day, I have to force myself to leave my house. I can't do it anymore."

Gavin felt his heart sink in his chest and bowed his head. He wanted to cry. "This is all my fault," Gavin said, shaking his head. "If I had allowed it with Nasher, he wouldn't have come after you or Mabel. I messed up, man." Gavin almost choked on his words.

Jamella turned her head to Gavin. She lifted his face up, so his eyes were level with hers. "No, it's not your fault, baby. It's that rubbish boy's fault." Her Bajan accent was at its strongest when she threw insults. Gavin loved it, as it made him smile. "You stood up for me. I will never forget that."

Gavin nodded his head and kissed Jamella. He savoured the feel and texture of her lips, knowing it might be a while before he had the pleasure of experiencing her lips again.

Jamella broke the kiss, and Gavin could already feel his chest clench in pain at the thought of not seeing her all the time. "Are you going to a new school in Hackney then?" he asked.

"No," Jamella said, avoiding Gavin's eyes now. Instead, she looked at the leaves in front of them. A ladybird was crawling on it. "I am going back to Barbados. My flight is tomorrow morning."

"Oh..." Gavin said, feeling like someone had thrown a ball at his head while he wasn't looking. He had thought she would just be moving to a new school in the borough. Not going back to Barbados. "You're not coming back?"

Jamella shrugged her shoulders. "I don't know, baby. Maybe not."

"So this might be the last time I see you?" Gavin could feel his voice crack.

"Yeah, it might be."

There was a brief moment of pause between them. Gavin knew he and Jamella were both thinking about the inevitable outcome of Jamella returning to Barbados and what that would mean for their relationship. Yet they were both too scared to verbalise it. Jamella then turned to look at Gavin.

She caressed his fingers and started another conversation.

"You know, you never told me something," she said, her voice barely holding together.

Gavin looked at her and raised his eyebrows. "What didn't I tell you?"

"Why you moved all the way from Brixton to Hackney?"

"Oh," Gavin said, caught off guard by the question. He shifted uncomfortably on the log and stared deeply into Jamella's light brown face with those soft lips and dark eyes. There was no point in hiding anything from her now. Gavin let out a sigh, knowing that he was about to reach into an uncomfortable part of his feelings, pull them out and display them to Jamella. It was a vulnerability he had only shared with himself when he was alone with his grief and tears.

"I was born in Brixton on an estate called Angell Town," Gavin started, looking at the sprouting leaves in front of him. "And I grew up with my neighbour and best friend. His name was Jamal."

Gavin smiled to himself as he said his name. "We had met in primary school when our mums became bare close. We started to do everything together and became like brothers, innit." Gavin closed his eyes for a moment. He could feel the ache in his heart.

Jamella rested her right hand on his shoulder. "It's ok, baby, if you don't want to tell me."

"Nah, I am calm," Gavin said, opening his eyes. "Jamal and I were supposed to start secondary school together in Brixton, but…." Gavin took a deep breath and readied himself to say the most challenging sentence he ever had to say, "last summer, he was stabbed to death in front of me. The boys who did it stabbed him once, and just like that, he was gone. I was right there when he died, innit." Gavin could feel himself shaking, and there was already a lump in his throat. All of his silent willpower forced his tears to remain inside his eyes.

"Why was he stabbed?" Jamella asked, squeezing Gavin's hands.

"It's a long story that I don't wanna go into," Gavin quickly said, not wishing to relive the memories of everything that happened after Jamal's murder. It was a wound that had not fully healed and might never. "After Jamal's death, my mum didn't feel it was safe anymore for me to be in Brixton. So she sent me to Hackney to live with my uncle because she probably felt I would be safer here with him." Gavin chuckled. "Which is kinda jokes, if you think about it, with all the madness that's happened with Nasher and me almost losing my life."

"Yeah. but your uncle did save your life, in the end."

"True say." Gavin went silent. He realised that, apart from his mum, Jamella was the first person he had spoken to about Jamal's murder since it happened.

Jamella now shifted uneasily beside Gavin. Noticing this, Gavin looked at her and he could tell that Jamella had something on her mind.

"I had an older sister back in Barbados," she started, looking up at the greying skies above the branches and leaves. "She was five years older than me. We used to play together on the beach, and she would always braid my hair, give me advice about boys, and we made dance routines to Destiny's Child songs." Jamella's mouth flipped into a smile, but then she bowed her head, and a sense of sadness washed over her. "But then she became very sick one day. She was only 17 when she died of leukaemia. Before she died, she gave me this bandanna." Jamella pointed to the pink bandanna she often wrapped around her head and looked at Gavin. "She always wore this bandanna, so when I wear it, I feel like I have a part of her that is always with me." Jamella then bit her lip and played with a curly strand of her hair, looking embarrassed. "I don't know if you have something that reminds you of Jamal that you keep with you? Does what I am saying sound dumb?"

"Nah, it ain't dumb," Gavin said, thinking about the torn Pokémon card being held together with tape. He tapped the breast pocket on his blazer where he kept the card Jamal had gifted him. "The people we lost left a piece of themselves that belongs to us and only us, you get me."

Jamella smiled at Gavin and nodded her head. "Yeah."

For a long time, Gavin and Jamella sat together on the log without saying another word. Shrouded by the leaves and plants, they watched the birds tweet and hop. Squirrels scurried across the branches above their heads, and Gavin heard the excited shouts from the boys still playing football. Someone had scored a goal. Gavin couldn't help but think, in pursuing revenge against Nasher, he had scored an own goal because now he was losing Jamella. Gavin turned his head away from her as the tears dropped from his eyes; he did not want her to see him crying.

Eventually, after ten minutes of sitting together in silence, Gavin and Jamella decided to head back. They walked back through the bushes, holding each other's hands. Gavin did not let go of her hand once as they walked to the bus stop. Jamella had to catch her flight early in the morning.

Once they reached the bus stop, they sat on the red seat. An elderly black woman in a brown jacket and white headscarf was sitting at the bus stop. Jamella sat on Gavin's lap, and they started kissing each other, ignoring the loud cough of disapproval the lady made.

Bus 308, heading towards Homerton, was coming from up the road. Jamella peeled her lips away from Gavin. "My bus is coming," Jamella said, her voice heavy with regret.

Gavin did not want to let Jamella go as she got up from his lap. They now stood facing each other, both of them holding back tears.

"Will you message me on Facebook sometimes?" Jamella said, her voice breaking as she looked into Gavin's eyes. Bus 308 had stopped at the bus stop.

"Yeah, I will. I promise."

Jamella gave Gavin one final peck on the lips and then hurried towards the bus. Gavin watched her get on. His eyes followed her as she walked up the stairs in the double-decker bus. Jamella took a seat at the back of the top deck. As the bus doors closed and the 308 drove away, Jamella turned around and looked out the rear window. She blew Gavin a kiss. Gavin did the same and watched the bus drive off down the road before it took a turn and disappeared from his view.

That day was the last time Gavin ever saw Jamella Greenwood. His first love.

Six months later

Chapter Sixteen

The Hackney Saiyans

August 2008

Shanice Campbell sat with a group of women at the Dogstar pub on Coldharbour Lane in Brixton. In front of her was a table filled with bottles of the pub's best house wine. Today was a cause for celebration; Shanice had officially passed her exams. She was now a qualified youth worker.

To mark the special occasion, Shanice had invited her friends to the Dogstar to drink wine and have a good time. Later they would head out to Brixton for a wild girl's night out. Just because she was nearing her 40s was not going to stop Shanice from enjoying herself, especially when life had given her the rare free evening.

As her friends sipped on wine and spoke loudly about their husbands, boyfriends and bosses, the alcohol loosening their tongues, Shanice remembered something. She had said she would call her brother before she started drinking. Grabbing her handbag and slipping away from her boisterous group of friends, Shanice walked over to the front door, pushed it open and stepped outside.

It was only 5pm on Friday. Brixton was not yet in full swing, but a few people were already walking into pubs and bars. Shanice took out her Nokia 6280 and speed-dialled Reece.

"Hey, sis," came Reece's cheerful voice from the phone. "Congrats. Big youth worker now, huh. I am happy for you. Always knew you could do it, you know. Dad would have been so proud of you."

"Thanks, Reece," Shanice said, smiling. "I just wanted to give you a quick call about Gavin. He's been living with you for some time now and is about to start year 8. So, I was thinking he could move back in with me? I've finished my exams now, so I have more free time. Also, things have calmed down a lot in Brixton."

"Sis, let me be completely honest with you. Gavin's been through so much already; I think he's finally settled down in Hackney. He's made new friends, and he's doing decent at school. I don't think he should move back to Brixton anytime soon."

Shanice contemplated her brother's response. Being a mother, she naturally missed seeing her son around the house and doing the wonderful things a mother does for her child. Shanice wanted to help him with his homework, meet his friends and iron his clothes in the morning. But Shanice knew, as much as she hated to admit it, that her brother was right. Gavin had found his place in Hackney. It was his home now.

"I hate that you're always right," Shanice said with a light chuckle. "So you don't mind him living with you for the rest of his time at school, and he'll stay with me every other weekend?

"Yeah, let's stick to that arrangement for now. I think that's what's best. And no matter what, you'll always be his mum. He knows you love him and he loves you."

"I appreciate you saying that, Reece," Shanice said, fighting back the tears, "it means a lot." She was silent for a moment before speaking again. "What is he doing now anyway?"

"I think he's off to play football in the park with his friends. Do you want to speak to him?"

"I am out with friends tonight, and if he's about to go and play football, he won't even spare me ten seconds of his time." Shanice chuckled and smiled to herself. "I'll see him next weekend. Tell him I said I love him."

"I will, sis."

"Oh, and Reece."

"Yeah?"

"Thank you for taking good care of him. We're both so lucky to have you."

"You don't need to thank me, sis. He's my nephew. There's nothing I wouldn't do for him. Now enjoy your night out but don't have too much fun. Remember your age, yeah."

"Oh please, your older sister can still buss some serious moves on the dance floor, you don't even know about me," Shanice said, laughing along with Reece. "Anyway, speak soon. Take care."

Shanice ended the call and put her phone back in her handbag. A mother's job was to protect her child, even if it meant making difficult decisions, so long as they were made out of love. Knowing that she had made the right decision to send her son to Hackney to live with his uncle made her feel less guilty about it.

Hearing her friends' voices becoming louder from inside the pub, Shanice turned on her heel and headed back inside, hoping her friends had at least left a bottle of wine for her.

******

As Gavin tied the laces on his football boots, he heard someone ring the doorbell of the flat. That was definitely Yemi and Kwesi. It was the last two weeks of the summer holidays, and a few boys from Kingsland Academy had organised a big football game at Victoria Park.

"Where did I put my shin pads, man? "Gavin said in a frustrated tone, as he began searching his room frantically. He overturned his pillows, removed his bedsheet and even looked under the bed. Still, Gavin could not locate his shin pads.

When Gavin removed his head from underneath his bed and stood up from the floor, someone pushed open the door of his room. It was uncle Reece.

"Your friends are waiting for you outside," uncle Reece said, looking at Gavin, who was still dishevelling his whole room to find his shin pads. "Your mum called as well and told me to tell you that she loves you. And don't forget you're sleeping over at hers next weekend."

"Yeah, yeah, I ain't forgotten, uncle Reece," Gavin said, looking through his laundry basket to find the elusive shin pads.

"Ok, I'll leave your door open. And you better tidy up this mess you're making when you're back." Uncle Reece walked out of the bedroom, leaving Gavin in his frustration.

Giving up on the laundry basket, Gavin left it alone and looked at the wooden shelf placed by the wall. Now he felt like slapping himself. His shin pads were right on top of the rack. Feeling like a doughnut, Gavin marched over to the shelf, stood on his toes, reached out his left arm and grabbed the shin pads. As he pulled them down, a card with tape around it fell from underneath them. The card landed on the floor. Holding the shin pads in his left hand, Gavin bent down and picked up the card.

A smile formed across his face when he realised it was the Charizard Pokémon card that Jamal had given him. After Nasher had torn it in half, Gavin had managed to tape it together. But the trading card was starting to deteriorate; its edges were bent, the front part was beginning to peel, and the colouring was slowly fading. Standing in the middle of his bedroom, Gavin held the card and stared at it. Then Jamal's voice came to him like the echo of a memory.

"Bruv, promise me you won't lose this Charizard Pokémon card. This is one of the best cards I have

given you. Charizard is one of the strongest Pokémon."

Gavin smiled and placed the Pokémon card back on the shelf. He no longer needed to carry it with him all the time. "I miss you, bruv," he said quietly to himself, feeling the ache in his heart.

After putting his shin pads inside his Nike bag, Gavin walked out of his bedroom. He closed the door behind him as he went downstairs to meet his two best friends.

******

"Do you have to wear that Arsenal kit," Kwesi said as Gavin stepped out of uncle Reece's flat, pushing his BMX bike.

Yemi and Kwesi were standing outside uncle Reece's flat, holding their BMX bikes. Yemi was dressed in a plain black top with two small holes at the bottom, faded grey shorts and second-hand football boots. Kwesi was dressed in the full Man Utd home attire with brand new football boots.

"Bruv, are you not wearing your ugly Man Utd kit?" Gavin said, smirking at Kwesi as he pulled his bike out of the front porch. "Don't hate, Big K. I am just repping my team, innit." Gavin bashed his fists against Kwesi's and Yemi's knuckles.

"I beg you man don't start arguing about Man Utd and Arsenal right now," Yemi said, rolling his eyes. "Let's just get to the park. The mandem are waiting on us so they can start the match. We're moving on some black times."

As Gavin mounted his bike along with Yemi and Kwesi, he saw three black boys in their late teens walking in their direction. The boys wore tracksuits and baseball caps. They were part of the Pembury Boys gang who lived on the estate but caused no trouble with any resident. Gavin, Yemi and Kwesi were calm with everyone on the estate, and everyone was cool with them. It was a real community.

"I hope you youngers are staying out of trouble, yeah?" said the tallest boy in the three-man group, who was called Clicks. His tracksuit bottoms were so baggy he had to keep pulling them up.

Gavin, Yemi and Kwesi bashed their fists against the three older boys' fists as they walked past them into another section of the estate. After the three boys had wandered off, Gavin, Yemi and Kwesi got on their bikes and cycled out of Pembury estate. As they peddled onto Clarence Road, a police car drove past them and turned into the estate.

"I swear I've been seeing bare boydem around the estate lately," Gavin said, cycling between Yemi and Kwesi.

"Yeah, bruv, there's been loads of robberies. And a few stabbings and shootings too. Oh yeah, did you lot hear what happened to Nasher?" Yemi said, looking at Gavin and then at Kwesi.

"Nah, what happened to him?" Gavin asked.

"He got bagged the other day, along with his gang. They robbed a betting shop in Stamford Hill and tried to escape, but police were waiting for them outside. From what man's hearing, Nasher and his lot have been kicked out of school permanently. They are gonna spend bare time in Feltham." There was a massive smile on Yemi's face as he said that.

"That's good," Kwesi said, pedalling a little faster to keep up with Gavin and Yemi. "We ain't gotta see his face and those stupid grills in his teeth anymore."

"That's true," Yemi said, chuckling. "But boys, listen up, we gotta stick together when we start year 8 in September. The ends are getting crazier every day. We gotta have each other's backs, you get me."

"Of course, fam," Gavin said, slapping Yemi lightly on the back while keeping steady on his bike. "We're the Crandale boys, innit."

"Nah, I ain't feeling that name anymore, you know," Yemi said, shaking his head.

"So what's gonna be the new name for our three-man squad then?" Kwesi asked.

Yemi looked at Gavin and Kwesi with a triumphant smile. "We're the Hackney Saiyans."

"Jheeez, yeah that's a hard name," Kwesi said, nodding approvingly. "What do you think, Gavz?"

"Hackney Saiyans, yeah?" Gavin said slowly, giving the new name some thought. Jamal would definitely have loved it.

"Yeah, I like it. I like it a lot."

Acknowledgements

Although writing this novel was a little easier than usual, I still had crucial help. Writing a book is rarely something you do in complete isolation. It is generally only possible to write a great or even merely competent novel with some external input along the way.

Firstly, I like to give a massive shout-out to my siblings. To my brother, as always, your football knowledge came in handy, especially regarding Arsenal and general football chit-chat. And to my sister for always providing small but constructive advice about story and structure.

Secondly, thank my editor and beta readers for the valuable feedback, which helped me shape the story and remove any elements that were not working.

Lastly, and apologies if this comes across as cheesy, but I would like to thank my dedicated readers. Not only for your patience as I wrote this book but also for your encouragement. I appreciate every single one of you.

Other books by Leke Apena

A Prophet Who Loved Her

(Out Now)

A black British romance novel unlike any other.

Set in London during the 1980s and 2008, it tells the story of two childhood lovers: Elijah, the proud son of a Nigerian pastor and Esther, a rebellious and bisexual girl with a beautiful voice who sings at Elijah's church.

They both grew up together and fell in love while surviving the racism and hardships of 80s Brixton.

After breaking up in the 90s, they find each other again in 2008. Elijah is now a successful pastor in a struggling marriage and Esther is a retired R'n'B singer searching for her estranged father who has mysteriously fled Nigeria.

Once they reconnect, they discover their emotional and sexual connection is still strong but their adult lives are a lot more complicated than it was when they were teenage lovers.

Is their love meant to be or must they say goodbye to each other again.

'A Prophet Who Loved Her is an enjoyable read with lots of love, humour as well as dramatic tension to keep you turning the pages.'

THE BRITISH BLACK LIST

ISBN: 978-1-6641-1234-6 | £14.

Other books by Leke Apena

Flavours of Black

(RELEASING MID 2023)

The highly anticipated follow-up to 'Flavours of Hackney', set 12 years later.

Fed up with being broke and overlooked for promotion, ambitious 24-year old Yemi Abimbola, with help from his two best friends, talented DJ Kwesi 'Big K' Adjei and the womanising Gavin Campbell - who both grew up with him in Hackney - decides to launch a Hip Hop, R'N'B, Bashment and Afrobeats club night called 'Flavours of Black.'

It becomes an overnight success, and suddenly the boys have a profitable events business. But it soon comes with challenges. Not only is their friendship tested when they start to attract fame and female attention, but the boys begin to exhibit some toxic masculinity traits which jeopardises their romantic relationships.

Soon, the three friends find themselves at odds with each other. As their personal lives descend into chaos, will Yemi, Kwesi and Gavin be able to transition from reckless young adults to responsible black men or will they lose their brotherhood and destroy their relationships forever?

Written in a unique and entertaining style, *Flavours of Black* is a funny and heartfelt coming-of-age story. It explores themes of brotherhood, toxic masculinity, sex and ambition against the backdrop of East London's alcohol-fuelled raving culture.

Keep updated about the book's release on
@urbanintellectualauthor Inst

Other books by Leke Apena

Secure The Bag, Not The Heart

(RELEASING LATE 2023)

Timon Abiola, a 30-year-old private hedge fund manager, is living his best life. He is engaged to a beautiful fashion model, lives in a penthouse in Mayfair and drives a Porsche. But when he loses a lot of money belonging to a dangerous client, his perfect life is threatened.

Desperate and fearing for his life, Timon is approached by Yinka Saraki, a 29-year old languages and psychology expert from his past. She deeply disliked Timon when they were growing up in east London as Timon and his friends used to torment her.

But when Yinka's boyfriend is kidnapped and the ransom to free him is hefty, she will need Timon's help to pull off a complex investment scam to deceive corrupt rich families into parting with their money.

As they grudgingly work together, travelling from London to Italy, Beijing, Dubai and finally Abuja, Timon and Yinka realise they share similar values around family, love and life. An attraction gradually builds between them, but as their mission becomes increasingly more dangerous and a mysterious agent from Mi6 begins trailing them, they can't afford to be distracted by their feelings.

They must secure the bag.
Their lives depend on it.

Keep updated about the book's release on
@urbanintellectualauthor Instagram

Do you want to publish a book?

As an indie author, I know how hard it can be to not only write and finish a novel, but the gargantuan effort it takes to put it out there in the world.

Sure, you can try and find an agent who will attempt to 'sell' your book to a traditional publisher or you can submit your manuscript unsolicited to a big publishing house. While I am not knocking either of these routes, their not the easiest and many great writers lose their passion for writing after receiving rejection letter after rejection letter from publishers and agents.

So why not go down the independent route? Where only your passion, talent and vision for your book matters?

At Urban Intellectual Writing School, I will help bring your book to life. I will help with everything in the book production process such as:

-Editing
- Book design
- Marketing
- Social media marketing
- PR
- And much more…

Let me help you publish and market your amazing book
To start a conversation, you can contact me via:
Phone: 07908073815
Email: adelekeapena@hotmail.com

Please leave a review

Firstly, thank you for buying my book and giving precious amounts of your beautiful life to actually read it and hopefully finish it.

As much as I love the freedom of being an indie author, it does come with its challenges. One of which is I am competing with mainstream writers who are backed my big publishers with even bigger marketing budgets.

It's for that reason that I please ask you to leave a review of this novel on **Amazon** or **Goodreads**.

Please be COMPLETELY honest in your review.

If you hated this book with a passion and thought it was the worse piece of fiction you'd ever read and you wasted precious minutes of your life reading it, please do write that in your review. I won't take it to heart. I love reviews, the good ones and the bad ones. All of it helps me improve my craft as a black British storyteller.

Thank you.

Leke Apena

Book Leke Apena for speaking events and writing workshops

Email: adelekeapena@hotmail.com